Honey Dipped
Secrets

K.D. McCrite

Annie's®

AnniesFiction.com

Library of Congress-in-Publication Data
Honey Dipped Secrets / by K.D. McCrite
p. cm.
I. Title
2016957421

AnniesFiction.com
(800) 282-6643
Chocolate Shoppe Mysteries™
Series Creator: Shari Lohner
Series Editors: Janice Tate, Ken Tate
Cover Illustrator: Bonnie Leick

10 11 12 13 14 | Printed in China | 9 8 7 6 5 4 3 2 1

"You know, Bertie and Aunt Cornelia are going to kill me." Jillian Green teetered at the top of a stepladder and tapped in the final nail. She smoothed the colorful plastic banner. "Is this straight?"

Savannah Cantrell took a step back and squinted. She brushed back a lock of dark auburn hair and turned to Jillian.

"Looks good to me. Kill you for what? Annihilating the orderliness of Belle Haven's kitchen, gouging holes in the bakery walls, or sneaking around behind their backs?"

"Ha, ha. Okay, they may not kill me, but if not, I think they may be the death of me." Jillian stepped onto the solid firmness of the floor and thanked Providence she hadn't landed there on her backside instead of her feet. Her red hair had escaped most of its pins and straggled around her face. She issued a hard, upward breath to blow it from her eyes.

"That mess I made in the kitchen this morning is enough to keep them occupied while we get the party set up," she said, eyeing the banner to assure herself it hung straight. "Those tiny holes in the walls aren't gouges. Besides, how else can someone hang a floppy Happy Birthday poster on this slick, high-gloss paint?"

She turned to Savannah and crinkled her face. "As for sneakiness, you cannot have a surprise birthday party without going behind some backs. I meant they are going to kill me for throwing a surprise party. You know how they like to be in on everything."

"Of course they do. They are practically Moss Hollow institutions, but it's tacky to prepare, invite, and decorate for your own birthday party. This we *all* know."

"Still, both women like to have their fingers in a lot of pies, birthday surprises included." Jillian brushed the dust off the front of her clothes, then nudged the ladder with her foot and watched it wobble. "That thing is dangerous. We need a new one."

"I'll stash this rickety old ladder in the storeroom." Savannah ran her gaze down Jillian. "You should go freshen up before the others get here."

"Right you are."

By the time Jillian had cleaned up, changed her clothes, and brushed her unruly red curls into a neat chignon in the ladies' room, most of the members of the Southern Sweetie Pies and the other guests had arrived. Bodies, laughter, and chatter filled one of Moss Hollow's favorite businesses, The Chocolate Shoppe Bakery.

While Jillian greeted the partygoers in the overflowing eating area of the small bakery, Savannah kept watch, peering out the back door's small window at the parking lot behind The Chocolate Shoppe.

"Think you pulled it off, Jillian?" Lois Freeman asked. Lois was not a member of the baking club that met every Sunday afternoon, but she was a loyal customer and a guest.

"I sure hope so."

"Quite a trick if she did," Wanda Jean Maplewood replied. "Bertie Harper and Cornelia Montgomery know everything in this town before it happens." Wanda Jean was always animated, and her thick knot of salt-and-pepper hair bobbed as she talked. It was common knowledge that Wanda Jean could no more keep her nose in her own business than water could run uphill.

"Did you say anything to either of them, Wanda Jean?" Jillian pinned an unhappy gaze on her.

Tittering and snickering filled the room, and all eyes were on the gossipy woman. Wanda Jean's mouth flew open as if outraged by such a notion.

"Why, of course not. You know me."

"And that's why she's asking." Lois Freeman's words sent everyone into gales of laughter as Savannah rushed into the room.

"Bertie and Cornelia just pulled into the parking lot. You should see their faces, mad as two wet hens. Jillian, if you were eight years old, they'd make you stand in the corner. As it is, you might be sent to bed without supper."

Jillian winced. The last thing she wanted to do was upset those two elderly women she loved so dearly, but this time, she had no choice. The previous night, she'd pretended to have a date with Bob Smith—a name she'd pulled out of the air and would have to explain later—and spent several hours at the bakery making and decorating a cake big enough to serve the Sweetie Pies baking club and numerous other friends. Savannah had assisted her, but Jillian had been adamant about baking the cake all on her own.

That morning, Jillian had faked an upset stomach and stayed home from church. As soon as Bertie and Cornelia left in Bertie's car, she emptied all the leftovers and tidbits from the refrigerator into other containers, leaving the unwashed original containers in the sink and scattered on the countertops and kitchen table. She'd deliberately spilled tea and dropped a raw egg. She'd taken pots and pans out of the cabinet to place them willy-nilly in unexpected places. In short, she had made a disaster in Belle Haven's normally immaculate kitchen.

If this party isn't a success, Jillian thought, *I will be sent to bed without supper.*

"Trickery was the only way I knew to keep them busy. I hope they won't stay mad."

"Hmm." Savannah twisted her mouth. "Maybe we should have sent some of the guests over to the house to distract them for a while."

"I should have thought of that. Maybe next time."

Jillian hurried back to the kitchen and quickly double-checked that a stack of pans successfully hid the huge chocolate cake she'd made the night before. If her grandmother and great-aunt went straight to the front without glancing into the kitchen, she could light the candles and roll the cake to a place of prominence.

Jillian had made this cake as a gift for the two most important women in her life. The success of the birthday confection, if it was as good as she hoped, would prove that Jillian had at last shed her novice baker's cloak. She'd had plenty of failures and humiliation since she'd returned to Georgia from California, but her determination to succeed remained strong. She often reminded herself that anyone who could succeed in the advertising business with a busy California firm, plus survive an engagement to the absolute wrong man, owned enough strength of mind and will to change careers. Now, she was pretty sure she carried the same baking gene that ran so strongly through her grandmother and great-aunt.

She had rifled through a box of old recipes until she found what she was looking for. The ingredients were simple, but the secret seemed to lie in how they were put together. *This will be the ultimate challenge*, she'd thought. The recipe was so old that the mixing tool for the batter was a spoon, not an electric beater.

She had learned the art of baking well, but the ability to increase recipes was something she had yet to master. For the party, Jillian had made four cakes, baking them in oblong pans, not layers, and then had placed them side by side. By the time she'd finished decorating the moist chocolate with thick milk-chocolate buttercream icing, no one would ever guess the cake was anything other than one solid sheet.

Jillian had yet to reach the heights of cake-decorating skills, but the simple, smooth finish she'd achieved satisfied her.

Keys rattled in the back-door lock. Jillian pressed herself against the wall at the far end of the kitchen, trying her best to stay out of sight. She crossed her fingers, hoping Wanda Jean and the rest of them had kept the party a secret.

Cornelia's strident voice pierced the silence as she opened the back door. "I'm not sure I will ever get that stain off the floor in front of the refrigerator."

"For goodness' sake, Cornelia, will you hush about the floor? A little tea stain on that one cracked tile can't make it look worse. Maybe some bleach will get rid of it. What *I* fail to appreciate was the dried egg yolk. Whatever could that girl have been doing? Juggling eggs?"

"Well, I thought she was sick. She *said* she was sick and that's why she didn't go to preachin' this morning. You don't fool around with eggs when your stomach is upset."

Both women were so busy complaining that they walked right through the kitchen without a single glance right or left.

"Well, Sweetie Pies," Bertie said as they walked into the front, "this is the quietest y'all have ever been—" Bertie's words ended in a gasp. "What in the world?"

"*Surprise!*" The word echoed through the bakery like a Georgia Bulldogs cheer.

Jillian hurriedly lit eight candles, one for each decade the twins had been alive. Pure white and a bit larger than usual, they were no ordinary birthday candles. Once lit, they sparkled rather than burned. The fiery colors they exuded reminded Jillian of the two women's intense personalities.

She moved the rolling table out from behind the barricade of pots and pans, and pushed it through the door and into the eating area. At the arrival of the cake, everyone broke into "Happy Birthday to You," singing it twice, once for each woman.

Bertie and Cornelia cast their happy, tearful, blue-eyed gazes around the crowded room.

"I declare," Bertie said.

"Mercy," Cornelia murmured, fingers on her lips.

"Who on earth came up with this notion?" Bertie asked.

"It was your own dear granddaughter." Savannah gave the women her brightest smile. "She's been working like crazy to make this party a success."

"And a surprise," Jillian added. "I'm sorry about the mess I made at home, but I had to make sure neither of you showed up before we had everything ready here."

"Mercy me," Cornelia said again. "Is that why there was dried egg yolk on the stove and ketchup spilled in the fridge and tea splattered on the floor?"

"Yes, ma'am. I am so sorry, but—"

Bertie raised one hand. "I don't care a diddly-doo about the mess she made, and neither do you, Cornelia. Jillian, honey, you threw us a surprise birthday party to beat them all." She turned to Savannah. "You had a hand in this too, didn't you?"

"Yes, ma'am, but Jillian was the mastermind."

"Of course she was." Bertie beamed. "And look at that cake. I can't wait to try it. Lenora, you outdid yourself on this one!"

"Don't give me the credit for that. Jillian did it her own self." Lenora Ryan, a large African-American woman, lived in the apartment above the bakery. She was Bertie's good friend and able assistant.

"Why, my goodness!" Bertie smiled proudly.

"Forevermore!" Cornelia said. "I knew she could do it."

Jillian's face grew warm. Their beaming faces were enough to melt her heart. All the hard work was worth that moment.

The twins approached the table and smiled so wide that Jillian was sure their faces would ache for an hour afterward. So far, they hadn't even noticed the gift table, piled high with gift bags and prettily wrapped packages.

"Try blowing out those candles," Maudie Honeycutt called.

"I've never seen anything like them. They're like the Fourth of July sparklers," Cornelia said. She bent from the waist, watching.

"I can't wait to have a piece of cake," Bertie said. "All we've had is a quick peanut butter sandwich after church. Jillian, that cake looks rich enough to have its own bank account."

The four cakes served everyone at the party, and nearly everyone took home a copy of the recipe.

"I am so proud of you," Bertie said to her at one point. "I knew a baker lived somewhere inside my city girl with the country heart."

Jillian laughed and hugged her grandmother.

"Don't leave me out." Cornelia said, reaching for her own hug.

The afternoon passed quickly, and no one seemed in any hurry to leave. The pile of birthday presents generated interest and plenty of admiration.

"I declare," Cornelia said, "this has been one of the best birthday parties I've ever had. Do you remember, Bertie, when we were fifteen and—"

The bell above the front door rang as a plump, elegant brunette in a bubblegum-pink linen suit and impossibly high heels entered, carrying a white ball of fluff in her arms. The woman blinked her huge green eyes at the crowd. A short, dapper man in an off-white suit and dark-rose bow tie followed her. He adjusted his round glasses.

The fluff in the woman's arms stiffened. A little black snout emerged. Alert black eyes shone like polished marbles, and tiny, pink-lined ears pricked forward. There was a barely audible growl, followed by a couple of hesitant yips, as though the dog was trying to find its voice. It barked at the room in general, then looked at each person and yapped at them. The staccato barks seemed endless, drowning every other sound.

The partygoers looked at one another and began to stir as if their leave-taking was imminent. Maudie Honeycutt, one of the oldest members of the Sweetie Pies, had two basset hounds and a shar-pei, so she should have been accustomed to dog noises. Her snow-white pixie-style hair gleamed in the sunlight pouring through the front windows as she got to her feet.

"This is too much, even for me," she said above the barking. "Good party, Jillian. I'll see y'all next week." A moment later, she was out the front door.

Jillian needed to do something. With a warm smile but firm intent, she approached the woman who seemed indifferent to the dog's yapping.

"I'm sorry, ma'am, but health codes dictate that no animals can be present where food is served."

The woman fixed a big-eyed stare on her as if stunned, then blinked her long, false eyelashes one time. She smiled, showing off dimples in both cheeks.

"Why, of course, honey," she drawled in an accent so thick it stood out, even in Moss Hollow, Georgia. "I am so very, very sorry." She turned to the man and shoved the dog into his arms. The barking hushed immediately. "You should've thought of health codes before we came inside, Bryce. Take Dipsy Doodle out." She dismissed him with a flutter of her manicured fingers and bestowed another bright smile on Jillian. "We call her Dipsy Dee for short."

Silence filled the bakery. The woman passed her brilliant smile around the entire group.

"Why, slap my grits and call them cheesy! Just look at all y'all having a party." She laid one hand with scarlet-painted nails on her chest. "I'm so sorry to have barged in, but no one was at the mansion." Again, her gaze swept the gathering, her eyes calculating behind the friendly demeanor. "I'm looking for Cornelia and Bertie."

"That would be us." Cornelia spoke from the decorated table where they sat. Bertie removed her party hat and patted her blondish-gray hair, but Cornelia showed no signs of removing hers.

The woman swept across the room toward them, hand extended. "Oh, my dears. It is so lovely to meet you at last. I'm Charmaine Rawlins."

She clasped Bertie's hand first, then Cornelia's, her smile never wavering, as if she expected them to know her.

"Of the Virginia Rawlinses," she added.

Bertie and Cornelia exchanged glances with each other, clearly puzzled.

Charmaine flung open both arms, her rings, bracelets, and necklaces glittering like an iceberg. "I'm one of your Virginia cousins!"

Bertie blinked. Cornelia's mouth fell open.

"Cousin?" Jillian said.

Neither Bertie nor Cornelia mentioned ancestors very often. In fact, they rarely talked about relatives at all. Jillian had always figured there must be very few.

Charmaine turned to face her, the friendly smile strained. "Yes, darlin'. Of the *Virginia* Rawlinses."

It took Jillian a few seconds to digest this bit of information, then she extended her hand and offered a smile.

"I'm Jillian Green. Bertie is my grandmother, and Cornelia is my great-aunt. Though I suppose you already know that?"

Unlike most Southern women Jillian had met, Charmaine wrung her hand with the strength of a lumberjack. No limp hand delicately placed against her palm here.

"Cousin Jilly! How wonderful to meet you." She dragged her gaze down Jillian's entire length, dimples deepening. "And, honey, aren't you just as pretty as a Georgia peach?"

Jillian stammered a thank-you, all the while thinking that this cousin couldn't be real. She seemed born of movie stereotypes, or even worse—television reality shows. Charmaine whirled 180 degrees on her ridiculously high heels, her eyes seeming to take in everything at once.

"I see cake and punch, and hats and gifts." She planted both fists on her hips and tipped her head to one side, a huge smile still curving her lips. "Y'all! Have I interrupted a birthday party?" She turned back to Bertie and Cornelia, grinning at them. "I am so sorry. I should've called first, but honestly, I wanted to surprise y'all."

"Would you like some cake?" Savannah said. As calm and lovely as a Sunday morning, she smiled and cut a piece, placing it on a plate. "This is Jillian's creation."

Charmaine took the plate, a plastic fork, and a pink paper napkin. "Oh, honey, this will go straight to my hips like it's made of steel and my bottom is a magnet."

Her remark broke some of the surprise and tension, drawing a laugh from the group. Jillian inwardly shook herself.

"How about a glass of punch?" she asked. "And what about your husband? Would he like some cake and punch too?"

Charmaine waved her fork and spoke around the bite of cake in her mouth. "Bryce is nothing but my personal assistant, honey. He doesn't need any cake."

Savannah met Jillian's eyes, asking a silent question. Jillian gave her an infinitesimal nod. Savannah laid some cake and a fork on a paper plate, filled a cup, and took it outside to the man who sat waiting in a midnight-blue Toyota Avalon.

Jillian turned to Charmaine and indicated the empty chair that had been vacated by Maudie Honeycutt. "Have a seat, Miss . . . I'm sorry. I didn't catch your last name."

"Rawlins."

"That's right. Of the *Virginia* Rawlinses."

"Yes." Charmaine's laugh rang out loudly as she sat down. "So what is this all about? Are y'all having a social, a party, or a Sunday school class?"

"We are the Southern Sweetie Pies," Bertie said. "We meet here on Sunday afternoons to visit and taste test one another's creations. But today—"

"We also exchange recipes," interrupted Lenora. "Some of us brag about our grandbabies, those of us who have them."

"Today isn't a regular meeting." Jillian glanced around the room. "These good people are friends and neighbors celebrating

Bertie and Cornelia's special day with us."

A man's voice at the back of the room spoke up. "That's right. Some of us aren't Sweetie Pies. Some of us don't even know which end of a wooden spoon to use."

The group burst out in laughter.

"I bet the gossip flows like moonshine in these backwoods," Charmaine said. She issued another braying laugh, and the group fell silent.

I wonder if she is being intentionally rude, or if she is simply clueless, Jillian thought before she tried to revive the lighthearted tone of the party. "I'd say we have our fair share of tidbits to tattle," she said lightly. "Moss Hollow isn't exactly a thrumming hive, but it's not drab and lackadaisical either. After all, what was the lead story in the *Moss Hollow Chronicle* the other day? 'Stray Cat Chases Skunk on Pine Avenue.'"

This had the desired effect, causing the others to chuckle.

"My niece is trying to be funny, so don't be misled." Cornelia tipped her head and studied the woman intently as Charmaine scraped icing from her plate. "I can't place you, dear, or any of the Virginia Rawlinses. I'm so sorry." She turned to her sister. "Do you remember them, Bertie?"

"I don't. But perhaps you'll join us for supper tonight, Miss Rawlins, and we'll talk about it then."

"Of course, honey! Absolutely." Charmaine leaned forward, green eyes sparkling as she moved her gaze from Bertie to Cornelia and back to Bertie. "As a matter of fact, there will be plenty of time to talk about family and old times." She paused, slightly flushed. "This chicken's come home to roost."

That caused Jillian's heart to drop. She forced herself to speak calmly. "What do you mean?"

Charmaine gave a single, big-eyed blink at her. Her dimples deepened. "Why, sugar, what do you think I mean? I've come home to my long-lost family, and I intend to settle into Belle Haven for a good long time."

A silence fell so completely, Jillian nearly heard her toes curl.

"I do hope you have room for me and Dipsy Dee," Charmaine continued. "And Bryce, of course. I simply must have Bryce nearby at all times, because I never know when I'll need him." She looked at Bertie and Cornelia. Her smile faltered, and her lower lip quivered, as if she were eight years old. "Surely there are at least two extra rooms in that big, old house of yours."

Bertie seemed at a loss for words, but Cornelia, who often placed her trust in the most unlikely and far-fetched arenas, found her voice.

"Of course. A cousin is welcome in our home anytime. Right, Jillian? Right, Bertie?"

Bertie nodded wordlessly, but Jillian harbored reservations. Just because someone turned up and claimed to be kin held no guarantee they were honest, or even honorable. Related or not, the woman and her personal assistant were strangers. Taking them in at Belle Haven seemed foolhardy at best, and possibly dangerous.

"I think the Southern Peach Inn would be a better idea—" she began.

"Absolutely not," Cornelia snapped. "Not when we have perfectly good guest rooms to offer."

Resisting Cornelia Montgomery was the surest way to make the woman dig in her heels, like a sulky teenager. Jillian gave in, at least temporarily, but she'd keep her eyes open. The first sign of any funny business from the newcomers, she'd chuck the pair out, with or without her great-aunt's blessing.

But before she could give her attention to this new concern, she had to take care of The Chocolate Shoppe. First, she needed to clear the bakery of the Sweetie Pies and the last of the curious partygoers who seemed in no hurry to leave. She almost expected Wanda Jean

Maplewood to take out her phone and start texting and snapping photos. A pleading glance to Savannah was all it took. She thanked God for a good friend who could often read her like a book.

"Hey, y'all," Savannah said, friendly and sweet as apple pie. "The party has been fun, but we've overrun our usual meeting time. Any folks we left at home are going to be wondering what happened to us."

"You are so right, Savannah," Lois Freeman said as she got to her feet. "Herbie will be calling the hospital to see if I'm there, likely as not."

"Won't he just call you on your cell phone, Lois?" Wanda Jean asked.

"Herbie and cell phones? Are you kidding? He'd rather use a string and two cans."

Jillian stood near the door and bid her friends good afternoon as cheerfully as she could. Her cheeks ached from smiling so much. A faint throbbing had begun at her temples and expanded as she thought about this newfound cousin and her entourage.

Even after they left the shop, most of the Sweetie Pies and guests stood on the sidewalk or in the parking lot, huddled as if they were about to launch into a game of football. Jillian knew they were trying to sort out the new development regarding Charmaine Rawlins. She turned away from the obvious gossip sessions.

"Cornelia," Bertie said, "why don't you take Charmaine and her friend to Belle Haven? Set them up in a couple of the guest rooms. I'll help Jillian clean up here and be home directly."

"Now, Bertie, no one should clean up after her own birthday party," Jillian said firmly. "I'll take care of this. You go with Aunt Cornelia."

"That's right," Savannah said. "I'll help Jillian. There really isn't much to do."

Cornelia looked around, crimping her lips. "At least this isn't like the mess you made at home. I thought we'd never get it tidied up in there."

"I already explained that, so let's not go into it again, please."

"And we forgive you," Cornelia said, nodding briskly.

"To see you happy and creative is the best birthday gift ever," Bertie said, "with the surprise party coming in second."

Both women beamed as if they'd awarded her a grand prize, complete with trophy.

Jillian kissed their wrinkled cheeks and embraced them, blinking back tears. "You two go on. I'll be home soon."

Bertie looked around as if still debating whether to go or stay. Her gaze halted on something a few feet away. Jillian turned to see what had caught her grandmother's attention.

Charmaine was industriously scraping loose frosting off the cake tray with her index finger and gobbling it down.

"Would you like another piece before you go?" Jillian asked, reaching for a clean paper plate.

Charmaine's face reddened. "Oh, mercy me! You caught me being tacky, didn't you?" She gave a schoolgirl giggle, as if trying to be innocent and cute. "We've been driving since early this morning and didn't stop to eat. But I can wait for dinner."

Savannah cut the woman a large piece of cake, put it on a paper plate, and handed it to her. "I'm sure your assistant would like more—"

Charmaine flipped one hand carelessly. "He's fine. He doesn't need anything."

Jillian wondered if the woman was as heartless as she sounded.

"Come, Cousin Charmaine," Cornelia said, extending a beckoning arm. "Bertie wants to get home and put her feet up."

"Why, Cornelia Amelia Belle Montgomery!" Bertie glared at her. "Not one time today have I said a word about wanting to go home and put up my feet."

"She's older than I am. That's why I know she must be tired," Cornelia said in a stage whisper as she linked her hand with Charmaine's elbow and led her to the door. "We'll be along momentarily, and you and your assistant can follow us to Belle Haven."

"Older by *two minutes*," Bertie growled as she turned to go through the kitchen.

"I was only joking," Cornelia said, following her. "A bit."

Savannah and Jillian snickered, watching the pair leave.

"I'll lock the front door, and then we can get started." Savannah snickered. "The age thing between those two . . . that's a new argument."

Jillian shrugged. "Not as new as you'd think. The age difference is merely something that is pulled out of the drawer from time to time for no good reason. I once heard Bertie tell Aunt Cornelia she had to go second at the ice-cream shop because she was younger."

Savannah locked the door and the deadbolt, then she grabbed a broom from behind the counter and started sweeping.

"Actually, it's rather nice that no matter how old you get, there's still a spark of the child."

Jillian stuffed the last bit of trash into a black garbage bag and tied it. "That's true. But sometimes, when those two get in a snit with each other, it's like kindergarten all over again."

Savannah laughed with her. "This was a great party, Jillian. As my old granny would've said, 'You done good.'"

"I couldn't have done it without your help."

"Sure you could have. You just didn't have to."

Within a few minutes, they had the bakery looking spic and span, ready for tomorrow's first customers. Savannah dug her car keys out of her purse and waited as Jillian ran one last critical gaze around to make sure everything was done. They went out the back door, and Jillian locked up.

"Bertie and Cornelia liked it, didn't they?" Jillian knew she sounded like a kid begging for reassurance, but the approval of those two old women meant more to her than anything else right then.

"They surely did," Savannah said patiently. "Did you see how their eyes shone? It was a fabulous party, Jillian, straight from your heart and hands."

Her words warmed Jillian's heart, but she still had to ask one last thing. "Even with the party crashers?"

"Even with. At least that woman brought something new to the celebration."

"Something new. Yes, for sure. But I have to say I'm a bit worried. Savannah, how could my grandmother and great-aunt be taken in by two perfect strangers? It's beyond all reason."

Savannah blessed Jillian with her gentle smile. "That's just you. You know how older people get about family and relatives and suchlike."

"It's not just me. How do we know that woman is family or a relative? She might not even be 'suchlike.'"

Savannah laughed, shaking her head.

"Oh, honestly, Savannah. How can you take it so lightly? For all we know, that woman and her assistant could be grifters, or jewel thieves, or moochers, or—"

"I'm not taking it lightly. But I don't think you should jump to the worst conclusions you can. Give Bertie and Cornelia credit for the good sense of their combined ages. Behind their gracious manners and hospitality, they're watchful. If something stinks in Denmark, they're going to smell it. Believe me. Go home, talk to Charmaine, and find out what you can about her."

"Then jump to conclusions?"

"Well, at least if you jump, then you'll have something substantial to land on." Savannah looked at her watch. "I need to go home and get changed. Call me tomorrow."

"Wait, wait, wait. Where are you going? Aren't you coming with me to help vet this situation?"

Even in the direst or rockiest situation, Savannah Cantrell was like a lighthouse, steadfast and comforting. Jillian wanted her friend with her that night to help her deal with the situation awaiting her at Belle Haven.

"I have plans tonight, Jillian." Her cheeks started to turn a little pink, and Jillian noticed instantly.

"You mean a date?"

"Sort of."

"All this time together in the last two days, and you didn't tell me."

"No biggie. We're going for burgers and that new sci-fi movie at the Cinema-Four."

"You called it a date. I heard you."

"Sometimes I think you have a thing against men."

Jillian said nothing.

"Of course, after finding out David Drake pulled that nonsense, I can understand."

"Nearly marrying an embezzling sneak is enough to put anyone off men for a good long while."

"Let's be thankful you found out in time."

"Yes, let's." Jillian put a lid on those painful, humiliating memories.

"I need to go." Savannah moved toward her car. "I'll talk to you tomorrow."

Jillian wished her best friend would go home with her, but she wasn't about to ask again. If she did, Savannah might change her plans just to support her. That's what best friends did for each other.

Best friends also do not mess around with each other's romances, Jillian thought. *Unless it's doomed, and the friend is too blinded by love to notice.*

Jillian knew Savannah's eyes were wide open in her relationship with James Wilson, though Savannah insisted they were "just friends." Whatever the case, Jillian wished them both the best.

She drew in a deep breath of the humid Georgia evening. The sweet fragrance of magnolias and gardenias mingled with the ever-so-slight scent of ozone. Long ago, she'd learned what that subtle smell foretold.

"Take a jacket," she called to Savannah. "I smell rain coming."

Her friend giggled as she got in the car. "Yes, Mother," she called back.

Wondering what she'd find when she reached Belle Haven, Jillian drove home with her stomach full of butterflies and a muscle knotted in the back her neck.

As a rule, Bertie and Cornelia wore their Sunday best for the Sweetie Pies meetings, but after the meeting, they normally came home, slipped into something comfortable, and relaxed for the remainder of the day. Sunday supper was always light—sandwiches or salad and soup—followed by an evening of *Masterpiece Theater* on PBS and an early bedtime. But when Jillian arrived home and walked into Belle Haven, she saw Bertie and Cornelia, still in their church clothes, busily preparing an evening meal.

The sealed lid on a jar of homemade spaghetti sauce popped as Bertie opened it. Jillian frowned as she peered into a steaming pot.

"Why are you doing all this work?" she asked. "You've had a big day. We've *all* had a big day. What's wrong with us eating those cold cuts in the fridge?"

"Because our guests haven't had an actual meal since breakfast," Bertie said.

"If you can call one of those McBiscuit doodlewhop thingamajigs 'breakfast,'" Cornelia said as she tore greens for a salad. "Why don't you fix the garlic bread, Jillian?"

Jillian was still up to her eyebrows with chocolate cake and punch from the party. The mere thought of food, even spaghetti and garlic bread, caused her uneasy, stress-filled stomach to lurch.

"I have a better idea," she said. "Give me a couple of minutes to freshen up, and I'll finish dinner. Put those salad greens back in the fridge, Aunt Cornelia. Bertie, you turn down the heat. Today is your birthday, and you shouldn't be working. I bet you haven't even taken time to enjoy your gifts. Go look at your presents, and leave the rest of this to me."

"There will be time to enjoy gifts later," Bertie said.

"But I—"

"Honey, I am too tired to argue." Bertie dragged her gaze down Jillian's somewhat disheveled appearance. "Go take a shower and change your clothes, then you can entertain our guests."

"Listen to your grandmother," Cornelia said, looking up from a pile of baby spinach.

The idea would have more appeal if the guests were on their way out the door to the Southern Peach Inn.

Jillian scolded herself for such uncharitable thoughts. Maybe she was just tired and out of sorts. Maybe her new cousin—*if* she was a cousin—and her personal assistant were better than first impressions.

"Where are they now?"

"We settled them in their rooms, so I'm sure they're resting."

"If they're resting, then they don't need to be entertained, do they?"

"I'm glad that dog of hers is asleep. I've never heard so much barking in all my life." Cornelia's face creased with a deep frown. "You should have heard him when he saw Possum. That poor kitty nearly wore himself out hissing."

"You know the Southern Peach Inn is ten minutes away. I'd be happy to suggest they—"

"For shame!" Cornelia looked as if she wanted to wash out Jillian's mouth with soap and then stand her in a corner. "We can't have our relatives staying in some dismal hotel when we have plenty of room right here."

Jillian planted a fist on each hip. "Have either of you considered the very real possibility that Charmaine is not a cousin? I've never heard you speak of the 'Virginia Rawlinses.'"

"Why forevermore!" Cornelia said, looking up from the cucumber she was peeling. "That does not signify."

"We're going to figure it out tonight," Bertie stated flatly.

"I see." Jillian relaxed somewhat, but the twins, while wily and astute in their own ways, were still a pair of sweet old dears who might be misled.

"Just because we're old, you shouldn't think we're ninnies," Bertie said, meeting Jillian's eyes over a cloud of steam as she lifted a lid to stir the sauce.

It's like she can read my mind.

"I'm only looking out for you, Bertie."

"I know. Now, go get cleaned up and be quick about it. No one wants to eat cold spaghetti."

By the time she'd showered and pulled on fresh jeans, a long-sleeved T-shirt, and comfy old sneakers, Jillian's fatigue had mellowed into a manageable weariness. She halted in surprise when she saw the dining room table had been laid out for an elegant dinner party, complete with a centerpiece of irises and delicate fronds of ferns. Most of the time, she, Bertie, and Cornelia had their meals in the breakfast nook off the kitchen.

Dressed in a tea-length, rose-colored, satin sheath dress and gray high heels, short brown hair lacquered in place, Charmaine bustled into the room. She had a book of matches in her hand. She gave Jillian a dazzling smile, dimples flashing.

"Candlelight dinner is simply a must sometimes, isn't it?" She hummed as she struck a match and held it to the wick just as the flame died.

Jillian watched her attempt to light the candle a few more times and then crossed to the sideboard and pulled a taper lighter from the top drawer. "This will make it easier for you."

"Of course. Thank you."

Jillian fingered the antique ivory damask tablecloth and eyed the Spode Fairy Dell china. She cast a furtive glance at Charmaine, who was happily lighting candles, before dashing into the kitchen.

Her grandmother stood at the sink, draining the spaghetti, a warm mist wreathing her face. She glanced at Jillian.

"Please set the table, would you? Then go fetch Charmaine and Bryce. Supper is almost ready."

"Charmaine is nearly finished with the table. She's lighting the candles. I thought you said we'd never use Great-Great-Grandmother Adele's tablecloth for anything other than Christmas dinner."

"That's right. It's too old and too precious to use more than once a year." Bertie dumped the pasta into a huge white bowl.

"We don't want to take a chance on anything staining those lovely linens," Cornelia added, somewhat primly. "That's why they're stored safely in the sideboard with the good china and the silver."

"Then why are we using all that for a spaghetti supper?"

"*What?*"

Without waiting for Jillian to say more, Bertie hurried out of the kitchen.

Cornelia stared down at the oil and vinegar cruet in her hand. "I'm as happy as the next person to have relatives visiting, and I didn't want to say much around Bertie, but I don't know about our cousin, Jillian. She seems . . . well, *pushy.*" She spoke quietly, almost as if talking to herself. She looked up and met Jillian's eyes. "The minute we got home, she started picking up things and asking the history of them." She held up one hand when Jillian frowned and started to speak. "I don't mean she looked at anything appraisingly exactly, as if she wanted to have it, but she seems to have such a lively curiosity. And my goodness, does she *talk*. A mile a minute, asking so many questions without taking a breath. There was no time to answer anything."

Bertie swept back into the kitchen, the tablecloth in her arms and an annoyed expression on her face. A moment later, Charmaine entered. Her eyes were wide and pain-filled. Tears clung to her lashes.

"I am so sorry. I never meant to drip candle wax on it."

"Candle wax!" Cornelia exclaimed in horror.

"I should be able to remove the wax with some ice," Bertie said. To Jillian's trained ear, the tension in her grandmother's voice twanged like an out-of-tune guitar, but to most people, she sounded gentle and sympathetic.

Charmaine twisted her hands and chewed on her lower lip as Cornelia studied the wax and Bertie pressed an ice cube against it.

"Great-Great-Grandmother Adele is rolling over in her grave," Cornelia fretted.

Charmaine gave a piteous little wail.

"No she isn't." Bertie glanced at the woman. "Please don't be upset. You didn't know."

Jillian handed Charmaine a paper towel as a fat tear spilled and tracked through the makeup on her cheek.

"I wanted to help. I wanted to make our first dinner together as beautiful as Belle Haven. I didn't know the tablecloth was antique." She sniffled and dabbed her eyes.

"Of course you didn't." Jillian poured her a glass of water. She did not add that the accident could have been avoided if Charmaine had asked first or refrained from pawing through the sideboard.

Bertie tossed the ice cube into the sink and scraped at the hardened wax with her fingernail.

"There. All done." She held up the offending clump of wax and then pitched it into the trash. She smiled at the tearful Charmaine. "Remember that trick next time you spill candle wax."

"But what about that stain?" Cornelia poked the cloth. "Look. A greasy blue spot right in the middle of the tablecloth."

"It will come out," Bertie said. "But now it's time for dinner. Is Bryce awake? He looked so tired earlier."

Charmaine sniffled and dabbed at her eyes. "I don't know. I made him keep Dipsy Dee in his room so I could rest, and I haven't heard either of them."

"Why don't you run upstairs and tell him dinner is ready?" Bertie said, then watched her leave. "Jillian, will you fold this tablecloth carefully and put it somewhere? We'll take it to Fresh 'n Kleen tomorrow. Rhonda has been in the cleaning business so long, I'm sure she'll know how to treat fine old table linens. Cornelia, let's get the food on the table."

"Dear, dear, dear," Cornelia muttered, watching Jillian as if she thought folding the tablecloth might break it. "I'm beginning to agree with Jillian. I think we should send them packing—"

"Cornelia!" Bertie said as if she were shocked.

The woman jumped and looked at her sister. "Bertie Alfreda! There is no need to raise your voice to me. I'm neither hard-of-hearing nor a spoiled child."

"Sometimes you seem to be both. Now, straighten up and act right. Charmaine and her friend are our guests. We will treat them as such. Bring the sauce."

With that, Bertie sailed out of the kitchen bearing the bowl of spaghetti.

Cornelia stared after her, her mouth in a thin line. "She has no right to talk to me like that. It's my birthday."

"Now, Aunt Cornelia," Jillian said soothingly, "nothing can be gained by being upset. We'll get everything sorted out. For now, though, let's enjoy a nice dinner."

"I hope you're right." Cornelia blew out a loud breath. "Bring the salad and the dressing, dear."

Jillian placed the stained tablecloth in a basket kept for items to be taken to the cleaners and put it near the back door. She wished she felt as confident as she had sounded. If someone had asked her why she had a niggling little feeling something was wrong, she'd be hard-pressed to give a good reason. It was something she felt in her bones.

Jillian figured they ate spaghetti off the good china because her good-mannered grandmother didn't want to embarrass Charmaine further. Cornelia failed to put on the cheerful face her twin displayed, especially as Dipsy Doodle sat in Charmaine's lap and whined until the woman gave her tidbits from her plate.

"This must be the servants' night off," Charmaine said, looking up as the dog licked her fingertips.

"Servants?" Cornelia echoed. "Harriet Fleming comes in from time to time to do some of the heavy cleaning for us, but we don't have a staff. More bread?" She passed the basket.

Something flashed through Charmaine's eyes as she glanced at Bryce, but he never looked up from his plate.

"I suppose good help is hard to come by." She bit into the buttery crust.

Without warning, Dipsy Doodle stiffened, growled, and then began barking, the sharp, staccato yips offending Jillian's ears. She followed the dog's focused gaze to Possum, the cream-and-chocolate long-haired cat who was arguably the most spoiled feline in Nathan County, Georgia. Possum stood, his back as arched as the dining room doorway, his blue eyes wide and fur standing on end.

The dog strained against Charmaine's arms, snarling and yapping.

"Bryce! Bryce!" Charmaine shrieked, shoving the excited dog into his arms. He held Dipsy Doodle to his chest and spoke in a soothing undertone. The barking ceased, but not the growling, the teeth-baring, or the hackle-raising.

"Dipsy Dee hates cats," Charmaine stated, as if delivering an announcement to the press. She pointed the rosy tip of her manicured index finger at Possum. "That cat needs to be put in a cage."

Bertie's mouth flew open, but no words came out.

Cornelia jerked as if someone had poked her. "I beg your pardon. Most certainly not."

"If it's allowed to roam freely all over the house, Dipsy Dee is going to be a nervous wreck." Charmaine's voice was hard, her expression stony.

Bertie gaped at Charmaine as Cornelia's mouth wagged open and shut as if she sought for words. She would find them soon enough, blurt them, and heaven help those caught in the fallout. One thing no visitor had ever done was demand Possum leave the room or be confined.

As much as Jillian wished her new cousin and entourage would find other accommodations, this situation was in desperate need of immediate diffusing.

"This is Possum's home," she said, holding Charmaine's gaze steadily. "Surely you understand that."

"But, honey dear, cats upset my little doggy."

"Then put Dippity Do in the garden shed outside." Cornelia had found her voice. "Possum stays inside as he's done since he was a bedraggled little kitten. Besides, that barking is giving me a severe headache."

"I mostly certainly will not put my dog in a garden shed!" Charmaine shouted. "And her name is Dipsy Doodle."

This sudden burst of passion and outrage caught Jillian off guard. With the three strong personalities who called Belle Haven home, the estate frequently had its share of mayhem and conflict, but a shouting match between her great-aunt and a stranger created an unexpected and unsettling dynamic.

"Raymond will never be locked up anywhere. Never!" Cornelia glared at Charmaine.

"Who?" Bryce said.

The last thing Jillian wanted to do was involve these strangers in her great-aunt's on-again off-again notion that Cornelia's deceased husband sometimes communicated through the cat.

"She means Possum," she said quickly. "Aunt Cornelia. Charmaine. Listen to me. There is no reason for either animal to be put in a cage or outside in the shed. The two pets simply need time to adjust to each other. And yelling at each other will only make things worse."

"Jillian is one hundred percent correct," Bertie inserted. "Everyone here must get along. Otherwise, we will make other arrangements." She pierced both women with her gaze. "Understood?"

Charmaine and Cornelia looked at each other for several seconds. The air in the dining room was electric.

"Understood?" Bertie repeated.

"Yes," they answered meekly in unison.

In the uneasy silence that followed, Jillian got up and coaxed Possum into the kitchen. She attempted to sooth the cat with warm milk and a bit of canned tuna. By the time she returned to the dining room, conversation had resumed, though it was far more subdued than it had been a few minutes earlier.

"You said you're from Virginia?" Bertie asked. Only someone who knew her as well as Jillian did would know that her smile was forced.

"Yes. Richmond, actually."

"Richmond?" Cornelia choked, sputtered, and coughed into her lace-trimmed napkin.

"You okay?" Jillian leaned forward, concerned.

Cornelia nodded. "Water went down the wrong way," she croaked, blotting the front of her dress with a napkin. "Sorry."

After a few seconds, Bertie turned back to Charmaine. "I've passed through your city once or twice, but that was long ago." She looked at Bryce, who ate his spaghetti with studied care. Dipsy Doodle lay quietly in his lap.

"And are you a native of Richmond also, Mr. . . .?"

"Bellingham, ma'am. Bryce Bellingham. And yes, I'm from Richmond." He shot a glance at Charmaine, whose smile seemed strained. "That is, not exactly. I mean, I was born and raised elsewhere but live there now."

"I don't perceive an accent of any kind. Where do you hail from originally?" Cornelia asked, fully recovered.

Charmaine's braying laugh hurt Jillian's ears. "Bryce has been in Virginia so long, he's nearly forgotten he's not a native. Right, Bryce?"

He nodded. "Yes. Right."

Jillian, Cornelia, and Bertie exchanged glances. Were these two keeping secrets? Charmaine certainly seemed to be keeping an eagle eye on her assistant, watching his every move, monitoring every word he shared.

Jillian spoke up. "I've never been to Virginia, but I hear it's lovely there."

"Oh, yes, it is quite lovely," Charmaine said, "but no more beautiful than what I've seen here in Georgia. Which reminds me . . . I do so want to visit that charming city Savannah. The photos I've seen, everything I've heard about it simply draws me. And of course, it's brimming with history."

Somehow Jillian found it hard to believe that Charmaine was a person who was interested in history. *But looks can be deceiving*, she reminded herself.

For the next few minutes, easy conversation flowed while the women chatted. Bryce kept his silence, but Jillian could tell he attended every word. The dog in his care snored softly on his lap, which Jillian thought was rather endearing.

After a while, though, when it seemed Bertie and Cornelia were content to merely talk around the elephant in the room, Jillian decided to approach it.

"Forgive our ignorance," she said to Charmaine, "but apparently we haven't studied our family tree as closely as we should have. Which branch is yours?"

"Oh, my dear," Charmaine murmured with her mouth full of pasta. She held up one hand as she chewed, then as she wiped her lips, and kept her hand in the halt position as she sipped several times from her water glass. She patted her lips again and shifted in her chair. "Captain Hoyt Belle, who built this gorgeous estate you now call home, was my great-great-great-great-great-grandfather."

"Oh?" Bertie and Cornelia said together, leaning forward. Their eyes brightened with interest. In Jillian's recollection, ancestry and family relations had never been a leading topic of conversation with these two women. She knew very little of Hoyt Belle. He served during the War of 1812 as an Army captain for the United States, and he'd been married twice. His first wife died of cholera quite soon after their wedding, and the woman he'd married a couple of years later was the mother of his children.

"My great-great-great-great-grandmother was his daughter by this third wife, Flora."

Cornelia and Bertie looked at each other.

"I've never heard of a third wife," Bertie said.

"No, indeed." Cornelia shook her head. "Why would that be, I wonder?"

Charmaine waved her fork with an air of nonchalance. "Well, you wouldn't have, of course. Hoyt was a well-to-do and respected landowner. Flora was the daughter of a local pig farmer." She raised her eyebrows and rolled her eyes. "She was much, much younger than Hoyt, and died in childbirth. Of course, she was quite beautiful." She sat up a little straighter and touched her hair as if she were looking in a mirror.

Why hadn't Jillian found something about this in that Moss Hollow history book she'd read a few months ago, or any other books or documents about the Belle family? That Bertie and Cornelia seemed more interested in this bit of family trivia than put off by it mystified her.

"But that doesn't explain why none of us ever heard of this woman," she said to Charmaine. "Family history is family history, after all, whether it involves pig farmers or not."

Charmaine flipped one hand as if the answer was simple. "Well, given Flora's youth and background, no one would have wanted to broadcast what was surely viewed as a scandal, even though the two were married. The baby—my great-great-great-great-grandmother—was sent off to Switzerland as a very young child, and I believe she never returned to America."

"That's probably why we've never heard of her or her mother," Bertie said.

Charmaine shifted in her seat and took another sip of water, then smiled warmly at Bertie. "Yes. That would be why."

"And the baby's name was . . .?" Jillian asked, watching Charmaine closely.

"Iris."

"Like the flower?"

"Yes. Beautiful name, beautiful flower." She showed her deep dimples as her eyes went to the bouquet on the table. "What an amazing coincidence that we have a centerpiece on this table with irises in it."

"Yes. Amazing." Jillian smiled and turned slightly toward Charmaine, holding her gaze. "Family history can be fascinating, can't it? So tell us, please. How did *you* find out about all this?"

Charmaine blinked at her once, as if she could hardly believe Jillian would ask such a silly question.

"Why, honey, it's common knowledge in the Rawlins branch of the family tree. The scandal is undoubtedly the main reason you heard nothing about Grandpa Belle's later exploits." She leaned over and planted a soft hand on Jillian's forearm. "Y'all come on up to Richmond someday, and I'll show you a whole passel of letters and old Bibles and artifacts. In fact"—she turned to the others—"I wish all of you *would* make plans to visit. We have a gorgeous old family home on Parris Avenue. Nothing as fine as Belle Haven, of course, especially with that gorgeous stained glass dome you have here, but it *is* beautiful, isn't it, Bryce? A snow-white Victorian, with lots of windows, pink gingerbread, and a gorgeous wraparound veranda where we hold parties in the summer. Oh, please say you will come."

"Perhaps we will one day."

"Honey, you simply *must*. This afternoon, I caught a little glimpse of your back garden. It's quite lovely, of course, but my garden at Parris House puts your little garden to shame, doesn't it, Bryce? When you ladies visit, you'll agree. Azaleas, gardenias, camellias, hollyhocks, roses . . ."

Charmaine continued gushing praises about her flower garden, ignoring Cornelia's frown. Cornelia prided herself on the strides she was making restoring the beauty of Belle Haven's gardens. To hint they were outshone elsewhere could have been considered a breach of etiquette, but Charmaine hardly paused for breath. She extolled the virtues of her house and from there returned to the convoluted subject of the family tree.

By that time, Jillian fervently wished she had never brought up the subject. Family history had never meant that much to her, and now it was even more complicated. Without realizing she'd done so, she tuned out Charmaine's trilling voice and found herself wishing to think of more pleasant things. *Ah, Hunter Greyson's bright-blue eyes.* From there it was easy to drift into thoughts of the local mortician's dark hair, his smile, his warm and gentle presence . . .

"What did you say?" Cornelia asked. Something in her great-aunt's voice yanked Jillian out of her daydream and back to the dinner table. Cornelia was staring wide-eyed at Charmaine.

"I asked if you know Arthur Fremont? Of the Charlottesville Fremonts. He's such a handsome fellow with that little glint of rapscallion in his eyes. He certainly knows you, Cornelia, and told me all about you and how—"

"Oh!" Cornelia gasped, her hand to her throat. Her flushed face suddenly drained of all color as she slid sideways and collapsed on the floor.

Charmaine shrieked and leaped to her feet. "What's wrong? Is she choking again?"

Dipsy Doodle was barking shrill staccato yips louder than Jillian thought a tiny dog could create. She knelt beside her great-aunt and thankfully saw the woman's eyelids flutter before opening completely. "Lie still." Jillian hoped her voice was soothing amidst the pandemonium. "Let's make sure you aren't hurt."

"Call an ambulance!" Charmaine yelled from two feet away. "Bryce, call 911. Make Dipsy Dee stop barking. Get some water. Get a wet rag. Bring me my phone!"

Cornelia waved one hand weakly toward her. "Don't call anyone. I'm all right."

Charmaine seemed incapable of remaining calm in a crisis. She hovered and chattered, flapping her hands, alternately scolding Bryce away or calling him back so that all he did was take a few steps in one direction and a few steps in another. Dipsy Doodle growled, yipped, and whimpered, squirming in Bryce's arms each time Charmaine's voice rose.

Cornelia groaned. "I'm all right. For pity's sake, tell that woman to hush."

"Calm down, dear," Bertie said to Charmaine. "The more agitated you are, the more upset your little dog becomes and the harder it is for the rest of us to help my sister. Go get us a cool cloth, please."

Charmaine scurried from the room.

"I'm all right," Cornelia said again, gesturing for everyone to step back as she sat up. "Stop fussing. Please."

She sputtered and fumed as Bertie and Jillian helped her back into her chair.

"Are you sure you're okay?" Jillian took the wet cloth Charmaine had brought from the kitchen and thanked her.

"Perfectly fine." She snatched the cloth from Jillian's hands and sponged her face. "I don't like having such a fuss made over me."

Truth be told, Cornelia had never shied away from attention, and she did like having a fuss made over her. But Jillian wisely chose not to point that out.

"Can I get you something? A cup of tea?"

Cornelia shook her head and blotted her forehead again. "No, no, dear. Nothing. I'm fine. But what with that wonderful cake you baked, and the refreshing punch Savannah made, bless your hearts, I think it's likely I've had too much sugar. You know I had *seconds* on the cake and *fourths* on the punch."

Her chuckle sounded forced, but the rest of them laughed with her uneasily, watching to see if she was going to pass out again.

Jillian glanced at her grandmother. "I think you should call Dr. Taylor, if he still makes house calls."

"He does." Bertie nodded enthusiastically and took her cell phone out of her pocket.

Cornelia grabbed her sister's wrist. "If you call John Taylor and make that dear man come over here in the middle of the night, I will never speak to you again, Bertie!"

"Then maybe I'll just drive you to the ER and let them check you out," Bertie replied.

"And it's not the middle of the night," added Jillian. "It's barely past sunset."

"I am not sick," Cornelia nearly shouted, "but y'all are making me ill with this deathbed nonsense."

Jillian eyed her great-aunt, noting her level of distress.

"Wait a minute on that call, Bertie," she said. "Aunt Cornelia, if we do as you say tonight, will you promise to go see Dr. Taylor tomorrow?"

Cornelia looked at her balefully, and for a moment, Jillian was sure she'd refuse. But at last, a long sigh escaped her.

"All right. Okay. But I've already told you what's wrong. I had too much cake and punch, and I got my blood sugar all out of whack."

"You do look pale," Charmaine said. "Doesn't she look pale, Bryce?"

He was rubbing Dipsy Doodle's fuzzy white head and ears. "Yes. Pale."

Cornelia shook her finger at the man. "When you reach eighty years, young man, you'll probably look pale too."

"Yes, ma'am."

She eyed him sharply, then said to Jillian. "I feel a little tired, so I believe I'll go to bed early. Jillian, walk me to my room, in case I feel a little light-headed again."

"Sure thing." She supported Cornelia with one arm around her waist and holding on to her with the other hand. "If you feel weak, lean on me."

"Shall I come too?" Charmaine chirped. "Here. I'll walk on your other side and you can lean on me too."

Cornelia stiffened and stopped. "No, no. I'm perfectly fine with Jillian. Thank you." She gave Charmaine a tight smile. Clutching Jillian's hand with a grip that belied any weakness, she walked with her out of the room, and they ascended the curved staircase. Possum came out from wherever he'd been hiding to follow them closely. He paused every couple of steps to look behind him and hiss.

Halfway up the staircase, Cornelia halted. Jillian looked at her in considerable concern. She tightened her grip.

"Are you all right? Feeling dizzy or weak? You want to sit down?

Cornelia frowned and shook her head. She leaned in. "Those people have riled up the haint of Belle Haven."

"Oh, now, Aunt Cornelia. I thought you'd gotten over that."

Cornelia reared back and offered her a look of complete bafflement. "I have no idea what that means. You thought I'd gotten over a ghost? As if I have some special way of controlling whatever goes on in the other realm." She glanced behind them and tightened her grip. "Look at Raymond. He's hissing up a storm."

"*Possum* is upset by that silly dog being in the house, not a ghost."

Cornelia huffed. "That may be, but he knows when something isn't right in Belle Haven." They resumed their ascent of the staircase.

"Yes, as you've said many times."

"Someday, maybe you'll wise up and believe me."

"Maybe so," Jillian said, full of doubt.

"You'll wake up one of these nights, eyeball to eyeball with a ghost, and then you'll come running to your old Aunt Cornelia, mark my words."

"I'm marking them. Now, here we are." She opened the door to Cornelia's room.

"Come in here, child." She pulled Jillian into the room, then peered down the hallway before closing the door with a quiet snick. "That young woman is annoying," she said in an undertone, as if she thought Charmaine lingered outside the bedroom door.

"I agree. But you and Bertie let her—"

"And that young man is completely henpecked." She slipped off her pale-gray sweater and handed it to Jillian. "I almost feel sorry for him."

"Yes, but you—"

"At first I thought he was stuck up." She gripped one bedpost for balance and stepped out of her shoes. "But I do believe she keeps him under her thumb so firmly that he has no mind of his own."

Jillian folded the cardigan neatly and put it in the sweater drawer of her aunt's cherry wardrobe. She picked up the low-heeled black pumps and set them on the floor of the closet.

"But didn't you notice—"

"At least he can keep that dreadful little dog under control." She fumbled with the clasp of her necklace. "Have you ever heard such a racket in your life? Unfasten this for me, will you, dear? I seem to be all thumbs."

"Sure. Turn around and I'll get it. Honestly, Aunt Cornelia, I didn't think it was a good idea for you and Bertie—"

"Not that I dislike dogs, you understand. And little Dipstick— "

"Dipsy Doodle."

"Yes, Dipsy Doodle is as cute as a bug, all white and fluffy, with those bright black eyes. But it's so loud. It seems to me if that woman can control a grown man the way she does poor Bryce, she should be able to control a little bitty dog."

"Here's your necklace."

"Thank you, dear." She hung the gold chain with its delicate cross on a little jewelry tree on her dresser. "I hope they go away soon. I can't imagine *why* anyone would want to stay with complete strangers, even if they are kin. I would certainly never go into a place I'd never been before, barge into the lives of people I did not know, and insist on being taken care of. And to suggest that we put Possum in a cage. Poor Possum, who has been nothing but a blessing to us all. Why, I nearly lost it, I tell you."

Jillian listened to her great-aunt's litany of complaints until Cornelia finally wound down.

"Remember that you and Bertie invited Charmaine, Bryce, and Dipsy Doodle to stay, when you could have simply directed them to the Southern Peach Inn. So in good conscience, you can hardly complain about them being in your home. It was your idea, after all."

Cornelia's mouth flew open. "Why, it was not my idea. Your grandmother cooked up this scheme."

Jillian took a soft, blue nightgown from a drawer in the wardrobe and laid it across the foot of the bed.

"I hardly think Bertie cooked up a scheme. The two of you agreed—"

"Go ahead. Take her side. No one ever listens to me but Possum. And Raymond." Raymond was Cornelia's long-deceased husband who, she declared, listened to her complaints and concerns and offered sound advice. Jillian bit the insides her lips and said nothing.

Cornelia glanced around, a panicked expression growing on her face. "Where is Possum? Has that dog got my dear Possum?"

She rushed across the room and started to fling open the bedroom door.

"Aunt Cornelia, Possum is right here, peeking out from under your bed."

Cornelia turned, spotted him, and her face softened. "Look at those eyes. Look at that sweet face. As soon as I take my bath and crawl into bed, Possum and I are going to have a nice long chat about how to get rid of that horrible woman and her nasty little dog."

Jillian inwardly rolled her eyes. Her great-aunt believed Possum had some sort of superpowers, but Cornelia Montgomery believed a lot of things that seemed peculiar to Jillian. Plus, she figured if Possum and Dipsy Doodle ever had a showdown, Possum would be the victor.

"Is there anything else I can do for you, or anything you need? Some chamomile tea? Some warm milk?"

"No, dear." Cornelia sighed. "Although, if you could think of a way to get those people out of Belle Haven sooner rather than later, I would consider it a blessing."

The woman looked so downcast for a moment that Jillian's heart stirred.

"Let's see what the next few days bring, shall we? Maybe everything will settle down. Maybe they'll leave soon."

Cornelia sighed again. She sat on the edge of the bed and began to peel off her stockings. "You're right, of course. It could be that they are merely passing through."

Jillian kissed the soft, wrinkled cheek and bid Cornelia a good night.

She lingered in the hallway a moment. Perhaps Charmaine and company were just passing through, but she doubted it. *Peculiar relatives don't just show up, then go away the next day.*

The following morning, Jillian woke to the sound of heavy rain. It pounded against her windows like the big bad wolf wanting to get into the little pig's straw house. She pulled the pillow over her head and yearned for more sleep.

Getting Charmaine settled in the night before had been chaotic. The woman was a wound-up talking machine, asking dozens of questions, hardly waiting for replies before her next barrage. Seeing her grandmother's tired face and the effort the older woman made to remain gracious, Jillian had taken over. She'd laid out Bertie's pajamas, ran her a warm bath, escorted her to her spacious bedroom, and demanded she retire for the evening.

"I'll take care of everything," Jillian had replied to each one of Bertie's protests until the woman had finally given way.

"I am rather tired," she had admitted at last.

As soon as Jillian was certain that Bertie was settled, she had dealt with the guests. Luckily, both were exhausted and had given in easily to her insistence that they retire.

That cool, rain-drenched morning, Jillian remained huddled beneath the covers for a couple of minutes before finally peeling the pillow from her face. She lifted her head, straining to hear any movement from downstairs, but the sound of heavy rain drowned out everything else.

Monday mornings were always busy at the bakery. Therefore, Belle Haven was extra busy as well. A glance at her bedside clock showed a blinking red 12:00, suggesting the electricity had gone out at some point.

"And that's one reason you have a smartphone," she muttered. But her smartphone was not on the nightstand or anywhere nearby. More than likely it was in the pocket of the slacks she'd worn at the birthday party the day before.

And that means my phone is probably in the laundry hamper. Phooey.

With a deep sigh, she threw back the covers and hustled out of bed and into her robe and slippers. Downstairs, the kitchen was unexpectedly dark and quiet. Had everyone overslept? Surely her grandmother hadn't crept around in silence, then slipped off quietly to The Chocolate Shoppe, leaving Jillian behind. And it was unlike Cornelia to oversleep, although maybe the circumstances of the day before had tired her out even more than Jillian first realized.

The smell of coffee and a tiny red beam of light on the coffeemaker signaled that someone had been up. The only other illumination in the kitchen was a small nightlight, but it revealed a white square of paper leaned against Jillian's favorite blue-and-white–checked mug.

Lenora and I can handle the bakery today. Take care of Cornelia and our guests. Don't forget to take her to the doctor. Make her go! —B.

Bertie had underlined "Make her go" twice.

Jillian reached for the cordless white phone on the countertop and punched in the numbers for The Chocolate Shoppe.

"Bertie, why didn't you wake me?" she scolded the moment her grandmother answered.

"Good morning to you too."

"Good morning. Why didn't you wake me?"

"I need you at the house more than I need you here," Bertie said. "Did you know the power went out sometime last night? We've not been able to get everything done on time."

"Then I should—"

"And the storm seems to be keeping people away," the woman continued as if Jillian hadn't spoken. "In fact, right now, Lenora and I are having coffee."

Jillian strained to hear any background sounds of activity, and she heard them. She wondered why her grandmother was pretending to be idle.

"Are you still there?" Bertie said.

"I am. But you've always said rainy days bring in more customers than usual. If no one is there, then why do I hear voices? And why did I just now hear the bell above the front door ring?"

"Bless your heart. I never said the place was empty. I said Lenora and I were having coffee and business is slow."

"But—"

"If you really want to help me, girl, then take care of our company. And get your aunt to the doctor. What I need is cooperation, not attitude."

Her grandmother's bossy tone took Jillian back three decades.

"Yes, ma'am," she said meekly, "but if you need me to come down there . . ."

"I'll call if I need you, but right now I don't have time to chitchat. You do what I said and no more sass."

"Yes, ma'am."

"I love you, sugar," she added, her tone more gentle.

Bertie was loving and giving, but she didn't always show her softer side. The endearment warmed Jillian's heart and boosted her drooping spirit.

"I love you too. Talk to you later."

Jillian replaced the phone and had just filled her coffee mug when something moved and crashed to the floor on the far side of the darkened room. She gave a little squeal and jumped, sloshing hot coffee over her hands and the front of her robe.

"Oh my goodness, you startled me." She shook coffee droplets off her fingers.

"I'm so sorry," Bryce said, taking a few steps closer so she could see him. "I was fumbling for the light switch and knocked something over. I didn't know anyone was in here."

"The switch is there, to the right of the door."

A moment later, light filled the room, showing her a rumpled man in a robe and pajamas. Without his glasses, he looked far younger than he had the day before. Dipsy Doodle stood quietly beside him, small head tipped to one side, black eyes bright and curious, white tail wagging hesitantly.

"I should have turned on the light when I first came in," Jillian said as he picked up a pan that he'd knocked off the counter, "but I saw the coffeepot indicator light and headed straight toward it."

Bryce offered her the first smile she'd seen from him. It came and went quickly. "I came down to let Dipsy Dee outside and to get some coffee for Charmaine. She seems to be coming down with a migraine today. This weather brings it on."

"I'm sorry to hear that. I'll fix a tray and take it up to her."

"Thank you, but coffee only, please; no food. She gets very nauseated with these headaches."

Jillian retrieved a wicker bed tray from a high shelf. She lined it with a pale-yellow linen mat. As her fingers smoothed the fabric, she recalled watching Cornelia tat the lace edging long ago. She had marveled how her great-aunt's nimble fingers had moved so quickly.

"We have some aspirin, and I believe there is some ibuprofen in Cornelia's bathroom medicine cabinet."

"Charmaine has taken her prescription medication, but sometimes it doesn't help very much." He picked up Dipsy Doodle and glanced around. "Where's the back door?"

She showed him the door leading to the mudroom. "There are some towels in a cupboard there to dry her off when she's finished."

"Thank you."

While Bryce tended to the dog, Jillian poured coffee into a delicate white china cup with saucer and placed it on a tray, along with cream and sugar. She was getting ready to carry it upstairs when Bryce returned, drying Dipsy Doodle with a fluffy green towel.

"She really is a good girl," he said. "She's usually quiet and well-behaved unless something scares her." He looked up. "I doubt she'd ever hurt your cat. I think she'd just bark at it."

"Oh." Until he added that last statement, Jillian thought he had been talking about Charmaine. "I didn't heard her at all last night."

He let the dog give a quick tongue flick to the end of his nose, then set her down. "As I said, she's usually very quiet." He smiled down at Dipsy Doodle, who trotted around the kitchen, sniffing everything, including Jillian's feet and Possum's feeding station near the breakfast table. Bryce looked up and met Jillian's eyes. "And she never soils inside the house, so you needn't worry on that account."

"She certainly seems happy right now." Jillian glanced at Possum's green food bowl and saw it was full. The cat was probably still in Cornelia's room. In the interest of peace and quiet, Jillian hoped he'd stay there.

"Is that tray for Charmaine? I'll take it up as I go." He reached for it.

"I've never had a migraine," she said as she handed over the tray, "but I hear they can be murder. I hope she feels better soon."

"She does suffer with them, poor girl." He clicked his tongue for the dog to follow as he walked to the doorway leading to the stairs.

"If you want to come back down after you've taken this to her," Jillian said, "I'll have your breakfast ready. What would you like? Scrambled eggs and bacon? Grits and gravy? Oatmeal?"

"Charmaine doesn't like to be by herself when she's ill, and I've already left her alone far too long." He held out the tray. "But if you don't mind adding another cup of coffee to this tray, I'd be grateful."

"Of course." She filled a second cup and placed it on the tray. "I could fix something for you and bring it up."

He shook his head. "Thank you, no. With these headaches, even the smell of food makes her ill."

"Oh dear. Well, I don't mind sitting with her if you want to slip off down here and get a bite or if you'd like to shower and get dressed."

"That's awfully kind of you, but no. I'll take this up now. Come, Dipsy Dee." He gave Jillian a quick, stiff smile and went out of the room.

Jillian bit her lower lip and frowned at the empty doorway. Bryce seemed so complacent. How many people would tolerate being spoken to the way Charmaine spoke to him before putting a stop to it? She completely disregarded his feelings and his needs. Why hadn't he walked out on her before now? What went on behind that placid face and silent demeanor?

She opened the blinds and sat at the table in the breakfast nook, cradling her coffee mug in both hands. She sighed deeply and stared out at the gloomy day. The thought of going back to bed tempted her, but if she actually did so, she knew one way or another her grandmother or great-aunt would find out. To those elderly women, illness was the only reason to be a layabout. Only spoiled prissy-missies indulged in such behavior otherwise. Jillian wasn't in the mood to be scolded.

Cornelia was not up yet, and that could only mean she was still not well. Although Jillian was glad her great-aunt was getting the extra rest, she worried about the woman's health. In fact, she worried about both women. Stubborn to the core, they were equally strong-willed but vulnerable to aging like the rest of humanity.

"They need a nice, long vacation," she said aloud. "And so do I." She allowed herself a little daydream about tropical islands with tall, fruity drinks and long, sunny days, then shook off the image before it could become a longing.

She was rinsing out her mug when Cornelia shuffled into the kitchen. With her blonde-white hair in disarray, her robe buttoned crookedly, and smudges beneath her tired-looking blue eyes, the woman seemed to have spent a restless, sleepless night.

"Good morning, Aunt Cornelia. Sit down, and I'll fix you some breakfast."

Cornelia sank into a chair without protest. She rested an elbow on the table, chin against her palm, staring at nothing. Jillian readily admitted her great-aunt could be as bossy and vocal as her twin sister, but unlike Bertie, Cornelia liked attention if she didn't always get her way. Disliking guests in the house definitely went against her grain. However, her drooping quietly this way shot Jillian's concern to a new level.

"Are you feeling worse, Aunt Cornelia?"

"I have felt better," Cornelia murmured.

"I'm taking you to see Dr. Taylor this morning, you know."

Cornelia sighed and said nothing.

Quickly, Jillian scrambled an egg and fixed toast. She prepared a strong cup of coffee for her aunt and set everything on a place mat in front of her.

"I'm not hungry, dear."

"I know you aren't, but you need to eat. Remember when I was a kid, you and Bertie insisted I eat when I didn't want to. Even if Mom said I didn't have to, you made me eat."

"That's because you were growing." Cornelia looked up and offered a smile.

"Well, maybe you are too," Jillian joked weakly. "You aren't upset because of that birthday yesterday, are you?"

"Of course not. Age means nothing, especially to someone like me." The strength and snap of the reply reassured Jillian, and she relaxed a little.

"Good. Then you finish that while I get dressed. As soon as you're ready, we'll head over to Doc's."

Cornelia fixed a soulful gaze on the pouring rain. "I'm not sick, Jillian, but if you make me go out in this miserable weather, I'm liable to come down with something." She shook her head and picked up her fork. "I'm not going anywhere today but back to bed."

"Now, Aunt Cornelia—"

Cornelia pinned a hard look on her. "I'm staying right here at Belle Haven." She cast a furtive look around the kitchen. "Where's that woman and her dreadful dog?"

"Charmaine is in bed with a bad headache."

"Oh?" There was more life in that one small word than in all her other words that morning. She sat straighter and used a fork to pierce some of her egg. "Well, I'm sorry she's ill, but at least we don't have to listen to her and that constant barking." She ate a couple of bites. "What about that fellow? Bryan?"

"Bryce. He's with her. Apparently, she doesn't like being alone when she's ill."

"She's one of those, eh? Well, obviously she didn't inherit the Belle family's hardy genes. Those genes are the ones that keep your grandmother and me as healthy and strong as we are at our age." She pointed her fork at Jillian. "You're full of the Belle genes. I can tell. You'll live to be a hundred."

By the time Cornelia finished her egg and toast, a banana, a handful of pecans, and three cups of coffee, she seemed almost back to her old self. Jillian couldn't help but wonder if her great-aunt's weakness had been brought about by their visitors. If that was the case, then Cornelia would fold again as soon as Charmaine recovered.

Unless I can persuade them to leave as soon as Charmaine feels better, but that's going to take time, tact, and determination.

"By the way," Cornelia said, meeting Jillian's eyes over her coffee cup, "do not call Dr. Taylor. I'm perfectly fine."

"Last night you—"

Cornelia raised one hand, palm out. "If you call that man, I will lock myself in the bathroom until he leaves. His time is too valuable to waste."

"But if you'd . . ."

Cornelia set her jaw. When Cornelia Belle Montgomery set her jaw, no power on earth would change her mind. Jillian blew out a long breath, knowing she was licked.

"All right. But you will let me know if you start feeling poorly again, won't you?" Jillian pinned her great-aunt with a look she hoped was more stern than exasperated.

"Of course."

A few moments ticked by as Cornelia sipped coffee. Jillian noticed the food in Possum's bowl was untouched, which said something about Dipsy Doodle's manners. Most dogs would have devoured a bowlful of food, whether it was for cats or people.

"Where's Possum?"

Cornelia put one hand on Jillian's arm and leaned close, looking into her eyes. "Possum told me that he'd just as soon stay in my bedroom while that dog is here." She sat back, a satisfied expression on her face.

"Possum told you that, did he?"

"Yes, shortly before I feel asleep last night."

"Well, then. Whatever makes Possum happy."

Cornelia narrowed her eyes. "Don't be sassy, dear. It's not only tacky, it's unbecoming."

Jillian tidied the kitchen while Cornelia sipped the last of her coffee. "So, you're feeling better, are you, Aunt Cornelia?"

"I am. That birthday cake you made was delicious, Jillian, but I do believe it upset my blood sugar and got my whole system out of whack."

"Yes, you said that yesterday."

"But yesterday I had not missed a good night's sleep like I did last night."

Jillian turned from the sink to frown at her aunt. "What is it about this logic that I fail to understand?"

"Simply that it took several hours for my body to readjust."

"Several hours and breakfast."

"Yes, that too."

"Three cups of strong coffee may have been more than you needed, Aunt Cornelia."

"Jillian, I'm going to go get dressed now. While I'm gone, see if you can think of ways to be more respectful to your elders." She lifted her chin and sailed from the kitchen, regal as a queen.

If Jillian's hands hadn't been wet with soapy water, she might have scratched her head. Maybe she should call Dr. Taylor anyway. On the other hand, if she called the good doctor every time her great-aunt said something that made no sense, the man would likely have had his own suite in Belle Haven long before now.

She made a fresh pot of coffee and went upstairs to get dressed while it brewed. Afterward, she carried a carafe to Charmaine's room and tapped lightly on the door.

Bryce opened it immediately, but only a crack. One brown eye blinked at her.

"Yes?" he whispered.

"I thought you might need more coffee." She held up the carafe.

He eyed it. "Thank you. Hand it to me as quickly and quietly as possible so the light doesn't reach her eyes. She screams if the light gets in her eyes."

Hastily, silently, awkwardly, she passed the carafe to him and found the door shut in her face, just as speedily and silently.

"Thank you," he whispered from the other side.

"If you need anything else . . ."

"I won't. Thank you."

She took half a step back and paused, thinking he might open the door to ask for a sandwich or perhaps something to read. Surely it was difficult for him to simply stand watch all day in a darkened room. She strained her ears for any sound from inside but heard nothing.

For a long, contemplative moment, she studied the closed door and wondered if something other than an ill woman, a caregiver, and a dog were on the other side.

The day was unseasonably cool for late April in Georgia. Jillian donned jeans, a white T-shirt, and a denim jacket, and then pulled her excess curls into a ponytail. Sitting crossed-legged on the bed, she opened her laptop and turned it on.

She typed Charmaine's name in the search bar and had several hits. None of the photos or any information she discovered matched the woman lying in the other room. She typed in Bryce's name and found no counterpart to his name. It seemed odd that, in this age of technology and ever-present social media, neither Bryce nor Charmaine had an online presence at all.

On the other hand, she knew a lot of people who preferred living life in a more face-to-face society. These people used the Internet sporadically, if at all. At most, it was a tool for their work. Jillian tended to be part of the latter. She wasn't a huge follower of any social media and preferred her magazines and books in paper form.

She typed "Captain Hoyt Belle" in the search bar and found nothing more than what she already knew. It seemed the local library had never uploaded their genealogy collection. She would go to the library and take another look at *The History of Moss Hollow.* This time, maybe she'd find what she was looking for.

So much for research at home. She closed her laptop, got off the bed, and slipped her feet into a pair of sneakers.

On her way downstairs, she paused at Charmaine's door and listened. Not a sound. Farther along the corridor, she stopped at Cornelia's bedroom and tapped on the door. When her great-aunt did not respond, she opened the door and peered inside. The bed was neatly made, the room empty.

She found Cornelia in her favorite chair in the living room, the CD player filling the air with soft instrumental music from the fifties. In a burgundy pantsuit, black flats, a bit of pink lipstick, and her white hair neatly combed, the woman exuded Southern gentility. A small basket was in her lap, and she busily sorted thread. She looked up as Jillian came into the room and dragged a gaze along her length.

"In my day, girls wore dresses, stockings, kitten heels, and earrings. And they kept their hair neat, even at home."

"I'm sure you looked a dream all the time." She said nothing of how Cornelia had looked earlier that morning.

"I did," Cornelia said. "And so did your grandmother." She rummaged through the basket some more.

"Are you working on something?"

Cornelia reached into another basket on the floor on her other side. She pulled out two plain white pillowcases.

"I'm going to tat edges for these. In fact, I'm going to tat edging for all our pillow slips." She shook them at Jillian. "There was a time when no self-respecting home in the South had unadorned pillow slips."

"I see." The fact that her great-aunt had a purpose that would keep her quietly in a chair for a while relieved some of Jillian's worry. "I'm going to run to the bakery for a minute to see how everything's going. Do you mind?"

"No, you go do that."

"Shall I fix you some lunch?"

Cornelia looked at her in surprise. "Lunch?" She glanced at her watch. "Mercy! No, child, no lunch for me. We'll call my late breakfast brunch, and it will hold me until supper." She went back to digging through her basket.

"I won't be long. Do you need anything while I'm in town?"

"Aha! Found it." She held up a skein of butter-yellow thread.

"No, I don't need a thing, dear." Then she lowered her hand, and her brow creased. "What about those people? I'd nearly forgotten about them."

"You mean Charmaine and Bryce? I think she's out of commission for the day with that headache. He's unlikely to leave her side, so I don't think you have anything to worry about."

The worry lines remained on Cornelia's face. Jillian felt a rush of tenderness and touched the woman's hand.

"If you need me, Aunt Cornelia, call me on my cell phone." She plucked the cordless phone off its stand and put it on the little table next to her great-aunt's chair. "I'll be home as soon as possible."

By the time Jillian left Belle Haven, the leaden sky had given way to a lighter shade of gray, and the rain slowed to a steady, gentle shower. She drove straight to The Chocolate Shoppe.

Jillian tried to dodge raindrops as she sprinted to the bakery. She entered the front door, and saw, in the far corner, a white-haired man reading a newspaper, and at a table near the window, Maudie Honeycutt and Wanda Jean Maplewood lingering over coffee. This was about as busy as the bakery ever became in early afternoon. Seeing her grandmother sitting at one of the bistro tables, a cup of steaming coffee in front of her, surprised Jillian, however.

"Bertie, you all right?" she asked in some alarm.

"Just a little tired. Lenora is cleaning the kitchen, and with nothing going on out here, I decided to take a break." She nudged a chair out with her foot. "Sit with me for a minute. Tell me what's going on at the house."

Jillian poured herself a cup of coffee from the pot near the end of the counter and grabbed an apple fritter.

"How is everyone doing?" Bertie asked as Jillian sat down across from her.

"Our guests are still cloistered. Bryce said the weather is likely what brought on Charmaine's headache, but I've heard nothing from either one of them for a while. Aunt Cornelia is feeling much better. She's up, dressed, did a bit of housework, and now she's in her favorite chair, tatting."

"Tatting? Why, Cornelia hasn't had a tatting shuttle and thread in her hands in a long time." She paused for a few seconds. "Years ago, when she was nervous or upset, she'd tat."

Jillian spoke quietly so the listening ears of Maudie and Wanda Jean couldn't hear her. "She seems all right, but having our 'cousins' in the house has upset her."

"I'm sure you're right. Cornelia often takes things to heart more than she should."

"Well, Bertie, I can't really blame her in this case. There is something . . . I don't know . . . off-kilter about these people. I tried to find information online about them and about what Charmaine told us last night."

"And?"

"I found nothing. I'm going to look into it further." She cut into the fritter and ate a bite, savoring the tender, cinnamon spiciness.

"Yes, do that, Jillian. If for no other reason than to put everyone's mind at ease. I'm prepared to give Charmaine the benefit of the doubt, but still . . ." She blew out a long slow sigh.

"I'm going to look at that Moss Hollow history book at the library. You know the one I mean?"

"In the rare book collection?"

She wiped her sticky lips. "Yes, ma'am. I've been wanting to look at it more closely, and now I think I should."

"Absolutely. Maybe it has something that will corroborate that wild tale she told us last night about Grandpa Belle and his third wife." Bertie glanced at the other table and lowered her voice to a near whisper. "Family secret or not, bits and pieces of it would have trickled down to the rest of us, I'm sure."

"I'm going to the library as soon as I leave here." She ate more of the apple fritter and found herself wishing it were twice as big.

"That's fine as long as you aren't gone from Belle Haven too long. Would Josi be willing to let you bring that book home from the library?"

"Not a rare book, Bertie."

"At least take notes."

"I will." Jillian stared hard at her grandmother. "Are you sure you're all right? You look really tired."

"I believe all this wet weather has gotten into my bones," she replied.

"This is where I feel it first," Maudie Honeycutt cut in. She held up an index finger as if pointing to the ceiling. "Right here in these two joints. I told Hugh last night we were in for a big rain."

"They ought to hire you over at the television station," Wanda Jean said, stirring sugar into her coffee. "You're probably better at predicting weather than they are."

Maudie nodded and the pair launched into a lively discussion of aches and pains.

Bertie's gaze turned thoughtful, a smile touching the corners of her lips. "I'm glad my sister is tatting. She used to say tatting helped to clear her head." She sipped her coffee and then murmured, "She should tat more."

Jillian drew her mouth into a thin line, stanching a saucy reply.

"How do you like your new cousins, Jillian?" Maudie asked.

"*Cousin.* Just the one," Jillian said. "Bryce is her personal assistant."

Maudie and Wanda Jean exchanged glances.

"That's fancy," Wanda Jean said. "I thought only celebrities had personal assistants. Is she a celebrity?"

"I hardly think so." Jillian popped the last of the apple fritter in her mouth.

"What does she do?"

Trust Wanda Jean to pry. Known to be as sweet and welcome as iced tea on a hot summer day, the woman also never hesitated to nose around anyone's business if her curiosity was piqued.

"She hasn't said." Bertie's tone plainly proclaimed this topic was not being discussed.

"Haven't you asked?" Maudie stared at her as if Bertie had lost her mind.

The bell above the door opened, and Hunter Greyson, Moss Hollow's handsome mortician, walked into the bakery. He flicked water drops off his black suit jacket and ran one hand over his dark hair. He spotted Jillian and smiled at her.

"Hello, Hunter," Bertie said. She nudged Jillian with her foot.

She needed no encouragement to greet him and sent her grandmother a quick frown. "Hi, Hunter. Would you like some coffee?"

"Sure would, thanks." He pulled out a chair and asked, "Do you mind if I sit here with you two?"

"Of course not," Jillian said. "Have a seat and I'll get your coffee."

"How about a Danish to go with it?" Bertie asked. "Jillian wasn't here to make the icing, which she does very, very well, but they're still good."

Jillian's face flamed, and she hurried to the coffeepot. How dare her grandmother tout drizzling icing as if it were one of Jillian's top marketable assets.

"She makes good coffee too," Maudie added. "Strong enough to walk by itself. Just what we need on a rainy day."

Oh, for heaven's sake.

"I'm sorry I had to miss your party yesterday, but happy belated birthday, Bertie." He handed her a small, square box wrapped in soft-yellow paper and looked around. "What's Cornelia up to today?"

"Thank you so much, Hunter." Bertie smiled at him and then at the box. "My sister was feeling a little under the weather this morning, so she's at home. And we understand that in your line of work, you can't always be available for every event in town."

Jillian set a coffee and a pastry in front of Hunter and excused herself for a moment. In the small restroom, she peered into the mirror. The rain had done her hair no favors. Her red curls sprang to life as if they had a mind of their own. She did her best to smooth them. Not much she could do about her lack of makeup. She'd hurried to the bakery that morning, and mascaraed eyelashes had been the least of her concerns.

All three women were gushing over the town's charming, personable mortician as if he were the only man in town. Jillian brought the coffeepot over and refilled everyone's cup, hoping to hush their effusive chatter.

"Look at these lovely earrings Hunter gave me," Bertie said. She held the small, sparkling studs.

"They're gorgeous, Bertie."

"They are smoky-brown crystal. I've never had anything like them before. Aren't they exquisite?"

"They sure are." She touched each chocolate stone with the tip of her finger, smiling and nodding. "And appropriate for someone who owns a place called The Chocolate Shoppe."

"That's exactly what I thought," Hunter said, grinning.

"Hunter Greyson," Bertie said in the tone she used to scold children, "you shouldn't have."

He grinned. "Special earrings for a special lady."

She smiled and patted his hand. "Well, I can't deny they're special, but still . . ." She gazed down at the sparkling stones.

Jillian filled Maudie's and Wanda Jean's cups, praying the exchange did not open a conversation about rings, engagements, and marriages.

"Thank you, dear," Maudie said. "You know, Jillian, I believe returning to Moss Hollow has done you good. And by being here, you certainly have done your part to pretty up this Chocolate Shoppe. Don't you think so, Hunter?"

Jillian groaned silently. Hunter choked a little on his coffee but set the cup down quickly and blotted his necktie with a napkin.

"I certainly do think so," he said with a quiet chuckle. "Although, of course, it needs no prettying up, not with all you pretty ladies around."

This brought about a burst of giggles, murmurs, and protests. Jillian replaced the coffeepot and took her seat. She heartily wished a busload of tourists would arrive.

A bus didn't show up, but a sky-blue SUV with five young people did. They entered, filling The Chocolate Shoppe with excited banter and laughter. Jillian started to get up to serve them, but Bertie grabbed her forearm.

"I'll take care of them. You stay and visit with Hunter."

As she moved away, Jillian muttered, "I don't see why she doesn't wrap me in colorful paper, tie a huge ribbon on my head, and hand me over. It would be more subtle."

Hunter's rich laugh rang out above the youthful chortles and drew curious looks from everyone. Jillian could hardly believe she'd spoken her thoughts aloud.

"I believe Southern grandmothers and their friends are notorious for matchmaking." He shot a good-natured grin at the pair sitting at the next table, openly eavesdropping.

"We just want what's best for Jillian," Wanda Jean said.

Maudie nodded enthusiastically.

"Well, honestly. You women." Jillian doubted she could blush any more than she was right then.

Hunter touched her hand briefly. "Don't worry about it. I have a couple of aunts and an elderly cousin who routinely try to set me up with every single woman in their paths." Three of the girls at the counter eyed Hunter and Jillian as if the pair were a couple of teens in the lunchroom. Jillian wondered why the kids weren't in school. Maybe they were older than they appeared. It seemed the more deeply she moved into middle age, the younger everyone else looked.

As if reading her mind, Hunter said, "Half-day holiday from school today. Teachers' meeting or something, I believe."

"I used to love school holidays," she said.

"So did I. And they were never long enough."

"Never."

Hunter shifted a bit in his chair, leaning forward enough to block Maudie and Wanda Jean's view of Jillian. "Listen, don't let them embarrass you with their good intentions." His smile was disarming. "I picked up the phone a couple of times to call you today, but I decided to stop by. I was hoping you'd be free Saturday evening. If so, how about dinner at Samson's? They've recently renovated and reopened, and I'd like to try it out."

After all the interference from the others and her own giggles and blushes, Jillian wanted to reply with a little class, like a lady. She cleared her throat.

"Dinner at Samson's would be very nice." Her words came out more primly than she intended. She smiled to soften them. "Thank you, Hunter."

She glanced across the room at her grandmother, who had raised both eyebrows.

Oh honestly, Bertie. Give it a rest. She supposed she and her grandmother should have a long, heart-to-heart talk at some point. Neither Jillian nor Hunter needed a push. They seemed to be doing just fine without outside interference.

"So tell me about your new relatives." He sunk his fork into the pastry.

"Relative," she corrected. "Just one. She's a talker."

"One of those, huh?"

"It's as if she runs on fully charged batteries. She has so much to say, and she wants to say it all at once."

He chuckled and took a sip of his coffee. The noisy young people exited. Their absence left the bakery unnaturally quiet for a moment before Bertie came charging across the room with the pot and refilled his cup.

"I don't think Jillian likes our cousin very much," she volunteered.

She sure has good hearing for an old lady, Jillian thought peevishly.

A thought seemed to shoot across his face, and Jillian spoke up before he could respond.

"It's not that I dislike her. I don't know her well enough to like or dislike her—"

"She's kin," Bertie said.

"Well, I know a certain embezzler who was very nearly kin," Jillian reminded her, "and we don't like him very much, do we?" David Drake had been Jillian's fiancé until she found out he was an embezzler. She had even lost her job in California due to the scandal. Now she didn't even like uttering his name.

Bertie gave her a sour look.

"I'm sure Charmaine is a perfectly lovely woman," Jillian said. "Showing up without a word of notice, and more or less inviting herself to stay with us—she surprised me, that's all." She refrained from saying more about Charmaine. For one thing, she didn't want to be a gossip. For another, she couldn't put her finger on any one real reason she felt the woman was a fraud, other than Jillian had nearly married one, so her radar was becoming quite acute. Right then, she wasn't truly convinced Charmaine remained abed with a headache.

"Who was the stuck-up man with her?" Maudie said. Glancing at Hunter, she added, "You should have seen him, dressed up and strutting like a banty rooster, looking down his nose at this bakery and all of us in here."

"The only way he could look was down his nose, he had it stuck in the air so high." Wanda Jean sniffed as though still perturbed.

"Bryce is her personal assistant," Jillian explained. "Actually, I believe he's probably a very nice man. If either of them is stuck-up, it would be her, not him. I think he's so quiet because Charmaine intimidates him."

"Intimidates him?" Maudie echoed.

Jillian clamped her mouth shut and shook her head. For someone who did not want to seem like a gossip, she'd certainly broadcast her judgment anyway.

"Well, he seemed uppity," Wanda Jean declared, "and if you don't want to be thought of as stuck-up, you shouldn't act snooty."

"And that dog," Maudie said. "Can you imagine bringing a dog into a place of business where food is served? What were they thinking?"

"He was a yapper," Lenora said, coming out of the kitchen, "but my goodness, I can't think when I've seen a cuter little mutt."

"That's no mutt," Bertie said. "I'm sure whatever it is, it's a fluffy, white-as-cotton purebred."

"Dipsy Doodle is a she," Jillian said, "and she barked because she was scared. This morning, she was sweet as could be. And she never made a sound."

"Still," Maudie sniffed, "dogs don't belong in a bakery."

Hunter studied Jillian's face, and an expression she couldn't read crossed his face. He seemed amused but was trying to hide it. Rather than pursue the subjects of cousins, dogs, and bakeries, he finished his coffee and polished off the Danish.

"Pick you up about seven on Saturday?" he said as he got to his feet.

"That will be fine."

"Great." He smiled at her. "I'm looking forward to it."

"So am I." She refrained from adding how nice it would be to have dinner together without well-intentioned scrutiny. On the other hand, it wasn't out of the realm of possibility that all those women might cook up some reason to have dinner at Samson's that same night, at that same time.

"See you then."

"'Bye, ladies," he called right before he stepped outside.

Maudie, Wanda Jean, Lenora, and Bertie all beamed like four brand-new headlights.

"That right there," said Maudie, watching him get in his car, "is the sweetest man in all of Moss Hollow."

"Yes, indeed." Wanda Jean nodded like a bobble-head dog ornament in a souped-up Mustang. "And is as available as the day is long."

Jillian stood. "Bertie, I'm going to call Cornelia, then run to the library."

Bertie walked toward the kitchen and beckoned Jillian to follow her.

"Honey," she said in an undertone, "I don't want either of us to think the worst of anyone. You know that. But . . ."

"But you have your reservations too, don't you?"

She hesitated, but then nodded. "Yes, I do. For now, let's be diligent. If you find anything that even remotely stirs your suspicions or unease, call me."

"I will. But, Bertie, since you feel this way, why did you let them stay at Belle Haven? They could have easily stayed at the inn."

"I know. But there's hardly any point in us talking about that now, is there? While I doubt either of those people could hurt a fly, I tend to think Charmaine has more up her sleeve than she's letting on."

Jillian agreed but didn't say so. "Don't worry. I'll look into it."

Bertie patted her cheek as if she were an adorable baby. "I know you will, sweetheart. I'll see you when I get home."

When Jillian called Belle Haven, Cornelia answered with her usual chipper voice.

"Everything all right?" Jillian asked.

"Right as rain," Cornelia said. "I've got the edging for the first pillow slip started."

"I meant are you feeling okay and have Bryce or Charmaine come downstairs?"

"I'm fine, and neither one has so much as opened that door. But you should see these pillow slips. Tatting must be like riding a bike. I haven't forgotten a bit of it."

"That's great. Maybe you can teach me to tat someday."

"Maybe. But I've never known you to enjoy crafting."

"And you never knew me to like baking either. Things change, you know."

"Umm-hmm." Cornelia sounded distracted and probably was.

"I thought I'd pop in at the library for a minute unless you need me at home."

"Not at all. I'm doing fine."

"Call my cell phone if you need me."

"Umm-hmm."

Cornelia hung up before Jillian could say good-bye.

Her run to the library proved nearly as fruitless as her online search. Her ancestor had done little more than serve in a war, build up a farm, and have two sons by his second wife. If he participated in notable heroics, built any monuments, wrote a book, or created a scandal, no evidence proved it.

Unless . . .

"If this was put together by the historical society, then there must be documents somewhere," Jillian said as she handed the book back to Josi Rosenschien, the librarian.

"Letters, family Bibles, all rare documentation about Moss Hollow and Nathan County history are housed with the historical society," Josi said. "I'm sure the volunteers wouldn't mind helping in your search, but the place is only open on Wednesday and Friday mornings, nine until noon."

Jillian had volunteered at the historical society long ago when she was just a teenager. Surely, she would have seen anything that referred to her own family back then. Wouldn't she? And didn't it stand to reason if such documents existed, Bertie and Cornelia would have known about them? Finding the truth about Flora Belle and her daughter might take more time than she anticipated. She winced.

"Rats."

"I know," Josi said. "So inconvenient. But there seems to be a dearth of volunteers right now. Esther Cole and Rita Powers are the only two manning the place these days. Esther's health is fragile, and Rita has her grandchildren every day but Wednesday and Fridays."

A shortage of volunteers to help maintain records of the past in a small Southern town? It seemed almost unfathomable to Jillian. Bertie and Cornelia might enjoy something like that, but Bertie was far too busy running The Chocolate Shoppe and it was all Cornelia could do to keep up with the gardens at Belle Haven. Snooping around in old records was more up Maudie and Wanda Jean's alley, anyway.

"I understand." She stifled a sigh. "Thanks, Josi. I appreciate your help."

When Jillian saw Charmaine the next morning at breakfast, she dismissed all doubt about the woman's migraine. She felt guilty for harboring those reservations in the first place.

With dark circles beneath her green eyes, Charmaine's face was a pasty white oval. She had made an attempt at grooming. Pink lipstick and a bit of blush helped to mask her pallor, and she'd pulled her hair back into a pink clasp. Her robe was neatly tied at the waist.

Bryce came into the kitchen right behind Charmaine. Dipsy Doodle followed quietly at their heels. The moment the pair sat down, the dog stretched out on the floor between them. Having survived yesterday on coffee and what Jillian suspected was little to no sleep, Bryce looked only marginally better than his boss.

When Jillian had returned from her errands the day before, the first thing she'd tried to do was to coax him from the room for a break and some food. He had remained firm in his commitment to look after Charmaine. Jillian hoped the woman fully appreciated his devotion.

"How are you feeling?" she asked.

"Better, thank you, honey," Charmaine said with a weak smile. "I'll be glad to get some food in me."

"We'll get you fixed right up. How are you today, Bryce?"

He looked up from adjusting the collar on Charmaine's pink robe. "Fine, thank you."

Bertie set a plate of sausage and bacon on the table, along with a bowl of grits, another bowl of scrambled eggs, and a basket of fresh, hot biscuits. Cornelia filled everyone's coffee cup.

Jillian wondered if Charmaine could tolerate the heavy Southern breakfast after a day of illness.

"Charmaine, maybe tea and toast would be better for you than—"

"Blessings, no! Once my headaches go away, I'm famished." She dove into the meal and ate as heartily as her assistant. By the time she pushed back her plate, color began to return to her cheeks. "Cousin Bertie and Cousin Cornelia, you two surely know how to cook like a house afire. I don't believe I've had a finer breakfast since the last I ate at the Culpepper & Hathcote Estates. Have you, Bryce?"

"No."

While Bertie, Cornelia, and Jillian nodded and murmured agreeably at the appropriate places, Charmaine went on at length about the Culpepper & Hathcote Estates, which turned out to be a bed-and-breakfast in northern Virginia.

"Now, here's today's agenda," she said when she'd exhausted that topic. "I'm going to take a nice, long shower and get dressed. Bryce will groom Dipsy Dee since he didn't do it yesterday." She gave him a hard-mouthed look. "Dipsy Dee needs to be brushed daily so her hair doesn't get tangled and matted."

Bryce said nothing, but Jillian spoke up. "To be fair, Charmaine, he hardly had the opportunity. He was watching over you every hour."

Charmaine narrowed her eyes at Jillian. "Well, that *is* his job, after all. It's what he gets paid for."

"You're fortunate, because he does it very well."

Charmaine stared at her as if contemplating a hidden meaning in Jillian's words. Then her face cleared, and she bestowed a quick, dimpled smile on her assistant, who had remained impassive during this brief exchange.

"At any rate, I want a tour of this magnificent old mansion today. I want to see where my ancestors walked and talked and lived. And you mustn't leave out a single nook or cranny." The last sentence she punctuated with a giggle. She cast a glance out the window. "It's still so horribly gloomy and wet out there, I daren't step outside for fear of triggering another migraine. But as soon as the famed Georgia sunshine returns, I demand an excursion of the entire estate." She leaned forward, passing a bright smile to them all. "Oh, it is *so wonderful* to come home. Because that's what this is, you know. A homecoming."

A little shiver crawled up Jillian's back. She exchanged a glance with her grandmother and great-aunt.

"I have to get to the bakery," Bertie said, getting up. "Two days in a row I've been late."

"I'm going to go clean up the breakfast mess." Cornelia scooted back her chair, grabbed her plate and flatware, and hurried into the kitchen. She returned moments later, pushing an old tea cart with a squeaky wheel. "As soon as I get the kitchen tidy, I can help you today, if you need me, Bertie," she said. "It's far too wet outside to do any gardening."

"You've not been well. I can—" Jillian started.

"Neither of you need to come in today," Bertie said. She met Jillian's gaze, and her expression said more than her words. "Lenora and I can manage fine. Besides, Maggie is there to help at the counter and with the cleaning up."

Jillian would rather go to the moon in a cardboard rocket than have to tend to Charmaine, but she had a feeling if Cornelia was left alone with Charmaine, this visiting "cousin" might upset the great-aunt far more than necessary. On the other hand, her grandmother looked tired.

"If you're sure," Jillian said.

"Doesn't anyone want to stay and give me a tour of this place?" Charmaine said. "I promise to take a shower first." Hearing that braying laugh, no one could have guessed the woman had spent the previous day silent in a darkened room.

Jillian tilted her head to one side, studying her. "I'm amazed at how well you recovered. I thought aftereffects of a migraine could be as debilitating as the migraine itself."

"They vary in degrees of severity," Charmaine said, losing her smile. "If I can take my medication soon enough, sometimes the headache doesn't get too bad."

Jillian was sorry Charmaine had been so ill, but she didn't trust the woman. She refused to let sympathy overcome vigilance and watched as the pair went back upstairs, Bryce one step behind, one hand out, as if to catch Charmaine, should she fall.

While Cornelia busily washed dishes, Jillian dried them with a plain muslin dish towel.

"Tea towels should have tatted edges too," Cornelia said as if yesterday's conversation had never been interrupted.

"Then you should do that."

"I will. What better way to relieve the pressure on a rainy day than to tat."

"Are you letting the presence of our 'cousin' get to you?"

Cornelia said nothing.

Jillian bent slightly to look at her closely. "Aunt Cornelia?"

"Does Possum have any food in his bowl?"

"I won't let anything happen," she said quietly. "I promise."

"Fill Possum's bowl. Look, there he is coming into the kitchen."

Whatever upset her great-aunt would remain untold, at least for the time being.

Jillian let out a long breath and turned to watch the cat ease into the room. His blue eyes seemed to probe every inch of space, looking for the unwanted dog.

"Poor kitty," Jillian said. "Come here. I have a tiny bit of leftover bacon off someone's plate you may have."

"It came from mine," Cornelia sniffed as Possum took the

bite delicately from Jillian's fingers. "You can bet Charmaine wouldn't have let a scrap of bacon go uneaten."

Jillian said nothing, hoping Cornelia would share what was on her mind. However, a minute later, Charmaine swept into the kitchen, the ever-faithful Bryce behind her, and Dipsy Doodle following him. The dog spotted the cat immediately. She froze, nose lifted and twitching.

"Bryce!" Charmaine snapped.

He snatched Dipsy Doodle into his arms. The canine ears were pricked forward and alert; the little black nose continued to sniff the air.

Charmaine put one hand to her head. "I cannot handle another animal fight."

"The two haven't fought," Jillian said. "They've never even gotten to know each other."

"I really can't deal with it." Charmaine held up both hands as if surrendering to something incomprehensible.

"That dog expert on television says if an owner becomes excited and agitated, the dog will too," Jillian said. "So if you stay calm, Dipsy Doodle will be fine."

"She's doing all right here in my arms," Bryce said. "Don't worry so much."

"Well." Charmaine sent Possum a dirty look, but she said nothing else.

"Shall we start the tour?" Jillian said with a sunny enthusiasm she didn't feel. The day was so overcast that she had turned on all the lights, dispelling as much of the gloom as possible inside the house.

"Coming with us, Cousin Cornelia?" Charmaine's smile was brighter than the crystal chandelier in the dining room. She held out one hand.

"I'm going to sit out this tour. I may develop a headache myself."

"Headaches in gloomy weather must be a family trait," Charmaine said with a giggle, almost as if she were desperate to fit in with her cousins. "I hope you're not coming down with one. I do want to see the mansion."

Jillian wondered what the clinical definition of a narcissist was. Charmaine probably filled the profile completely.

"Aunt Cornelia, shall I bring you some tea, or a cool cloth, or some aspirin?"

"Nothing, dear. Just a nice lie-down. Come along, Possum. Here, kitty, kitty."

Possum, fur fluffed in agitation, twitched his tail. With a hiss at the visiting trio, he trotted across the room with his tail and nose high in the air.

"Before we get started, let me tell you that we've done a lot of renovations to Belle Haven in the past few months. Some was done by a contractor, but we've also had a lot of help from the Sweetie Pies. They're some of the women you met at The Chocolate Shoppe on Sunday."

"What is the purpose of your little club?"

"Mostly social, but it's also a great way to share recipes and baking tips. We also taste-test one another's creations and frequently provide baked goods for various charity events."

Charmaine looked completely bored.

"Well, then," Jillian said brightly, trying to infuse some enthusiasm into the day, "you've already seen the kitchen, so let's not even—"

"No no, Cousin Jilly!" Charmaine grabbed her forearm and squeezed. "Land of Goshen, honey, we want to see it *all*. From the garage to the basement to the attic!" She let go of Jillian and extended both arms upward. "And the gardens too, when the ground dries."

I really don't like being called "Jilly," Jillian thought. *And "Land o' Goshen"? It's been years since I've heard that one.*

If they waited until the ground dried out, they might be staying another week or two, even longer, if the rain continued. Jillian's heart sank, but she kept her smile in place.

"We don't have a basement, but there's an old root cellar in the back." She paused for either to comment, but Bryce remained silent and Charmaine grinned eagerly. "So, bearing in mind that you want to 'see it all,' let's go through the kitchen and start at the porte cochere. We'll begin the tour there."

Charmaine's plump face crinkled. "Porte cochure? What's that, honey?"

How could someone with generations of wealthy Southern ancestors not know what a porte cochere was?

"Back in the day, all mansions had a porte cochere," Jillian said. "It was a covered place where vehicles stopped to let passengers alight. We use it as a carport now. Since it's outside, you can peek at it through the back door."

A light frown flashed across Charmaine's face, and she made a dismissive gesture with one hand. "Oh well, that. Pffft. Let's see everything else, then."

Charmaine's sharp eyes took in every tiny detail in every room, lingering from time to time as if certain areas or objects held great importance to her. Jillian wondered if the woman was assessing the collectibles and their value. In the foyer, Charmaine squinted up at the stained glass of Belle Haven's domed skylight.

"Will we get a close-up of *that*?"

"On the third floor, yes."

Charmaine frowned again and lowered her head. "It's almost like looking straight into the sun, isn't it?"

"With all the gold-colored glass, it is rather sunny," Jillian said. "If it bothers your eyes or makes your head hurt, we can go up there another time."

"No, no, I'm fine." Was there the slightest edge of a martyr's tone in her voice? "Bryce will fetch my medicine if I need it. Lead on, Cousin Jilly."

Jillian led them past the curved staircase to a set of closed mahogany double doors.

"Please excuse the dust and disarray in this room. None of us has done much of anything in here." She opened the doors and stepped aside, letting the visiting trio enter.

"A library," Bryce said, his eyes lighting up for the first time since Jillian had met him. His gaze took in the cold fireplace, the shabby overstuffed leather furniture, the faded old rugs, and two stories full of shelves stuffed with books.

"You have any family history in here?" Charmaine asked.

"If we did, I'm sure I'd know about it. These are books collected by various family members over the years. Bertie bought that set of encyclopedias for me when I was in high school. These days, all that information is online—"

"Nothing so boring as a bunch of old books." Charmaine ran her critical eyes over the room, pausing, probing, moving on before yawning and waving one hand dismissively. "Let's see the rest of the place." She moved to the door, but Bryce stood still, looking around, a half smile on his face.

"Are you a booklover?" Jillian asked him.

"Oh, yes. I once had plans to be a librarian, but—"

"Bryce!" Charmaine's voice was as sharp as the crack of a whip.

"Feel free to come back in here and enjoy the books later," Jillian said. "If you can stand the dust, that is."

"Thank you. I will, if I have the chance." He scurried toward Charmaine.

Jillian doubted he'd ever have the chance, unless it was in the middle of the night while Charmaine was fast asleep.

On the second floor, Jillian showed them the unused

apartment near the back. It held long unused mid-century modern furniture.

"I believe these rooms were added on as the butler's quarters, probably about the turn of the century. The twentieth century, that is."

Once again, Charmaine's eyes seemed to miss nothing. At one point, she turned to Bryce and pinned a hard stare on him. He blinked, but his face remained impassive.

"Why does no one live here, Cousin Jilly?" she asked as she left the apartment. "There seems to be plenty of space, and it isn't in too bad of shape. Get someone to clean and scrub it, and it could be quite adequate."

"Adequate? For what?" Jillian had a feeling she knew the answer to that, and dread filled her.

"For living, of course. You have several bedrooms here in Belle Haven, but that's all they are. Bedrooms with small en suite bathrooms." She met Jillian's eyes, then her face softened and she giggled. "What if you were to get married? Wouldn't you want your own apartment, away from the old ladies? They are perfectly sweet old dears, but, oh, my stars and stripes! You wouldn't want them underfoot all the time, especially when you're a newlywed."

Maybe Charmaine wasn't hinting at a plan to move into the apartment after all.

"I have no plans to be a newlywed anytime soon," Jillian said. The moment the words left her mouth, she winced inwardly. What if Charmaine took her words as a backhanded invitation to move in?

Charmaine glanced at Jillian's curly red hair. "You could be attractive enough. Don't give up hope."

Jillian saw no good reason to discuss her looks or matrimonial intentions, or lack thereof, with anyone.

"Let's continue with the tour. Here's the crafting room." She stepped inside, and the other two followed.

The tiny room had been outfitted with shelves, drawers, and cubbyholes on every wall. Yarns, threads, and fabrics of all colors, weights, and weaves were in abundance, but none of the busy women of Belle Haven had spent as much time in the room as they wanted to. Bertie enjoyed knitting but preferred to bake. It had been years since Jillian had picked up an embroidery needle and hoop. Years ago, Cornelia had done some quilting, but Jillian couldn't remember the last time she'd heard her great-aunt mention quilting patterns.

She thought of Cornelia's nimble fingers as the woman had worked on her tatting the day before. Maybe someday, when life slowed down a little, she'd ask Aunt Cornelia to teach her to tat.

"Do either of you do any kind of needlework?"

Bryce shook his head.

"Not me. I'm all thumbs." Charmaine's glance was cursory and screamed with disinterest. She looked across the corridor. "What's that room?"

Before Jillian could reply, she charged to Jillian's closed bedroom door and threw it open. Without an "Excuse me" or "May I?" she walked in and looked around. Bryce lingered at the door.

"This is my bedroom," Jillian said.

"Yes," she replied with a sigh. "I figured."

"Is there something about my chiffonier you find particularly interesting?" Jillian asked as Charmaine leaned near the piece, touching one of the top drawer pulls.

Charmaine yanked her hand back and delicately laid it against her chest. "Oh, no, honey. I've never seen one quite like it before." She took the dog from Bryce as if needing something to touch to keep her hands busy.

Jillian eyed the rather shabby chest of drawers and saw

nothing interesting about the scarred top and plain surface. Five drawers and a mirror on top. Old, yes. Antique, maybe. Collectible, probably not.

Bryce had said very little throughout the tour, although, like Charmaine, his gaze seemed to miss nothing.

"Excuse me for saying so, Cousin Jilly," Charmaine said as she walked out of the room, "but Belle Haven isn't very . . . interesting, is it? I expected to see, oh, I don't know, mementos of the past everywhere."

"This isn't a museum, Charmaine. We live here."

"Yes, honey, I understand. But it is a rather dull place to live, isn't it?" Her gaze landed on Cornelia's bedroom door.

Jillian headed her off before the woman could intrude on her great-aunt's privacy. "This is Aunt Cornelia's room."

"Oh, goody! I bet she has some great old stuff—"

She stepped between the door and Charmaine. "We won't disturb her."

"Oh, but—"

"No one disturbed you yesterday. Let's give Aunt Cornelia the same consideration."

Annoyance flashed across Charmaine's face, but she quickly hid it behind a toothy smile.

"Of course, honey. I'll look in there later."

Over my dead body.

Jillian held the woman's gaze until Charmaine looked away, her fake smile still huge on her face.

"Shall we go up to the third floor now?" Jillian suggested.

"Oh, the attic!" Charmaine's irritation evaporated, and her smile turned genuine. She clapped her hands. "I do love attics. They are so full of interesting things."

"Perhaps this one will please you then, but what about the light from the stained glass? Are you up to facing it?"

"I'm fine. I simply will not look at it directly. Lead on, Cousin Jilly."

If she calls me "Cousin Jilly" one more time, I may scream.

"Would you like to get your medicine while we're near your room?"

"I'm fine," Charmaine snapped. "I told you already that Bryce can get it for me, if I need it."

Ignoring Charmaine's curt response, Jillian looked at Bryce, who gave her the slightest nod.

"All right, then. This way."

Although Jillian had done some cleaning and organizing of the third-floor rooms a few months earlier, dust had returned. It lay like a soft film over everything when she turned on the overhead lights.

"I apologize for yet more dust," she said. "We rarely come up here, so this is mostly storage."

"Oh!" Charmaine said in a voice that dripped with surprise. "I thought . . ."

"You thought what?"

Charmaine ran her gaze across the huge room. Old woven rugs had been rolled up and now leaned against the wall near an old, dismantled bed frame. Clothing from several bygone eras hung on a long rod along one wall. The woman walked around the dusty gallery, her glance bypassing the old memorabilia she'd been whining to see earlier.

"I was hoping to see more family mementos. Letters, pictures, diaries. Something that I might recognize from my own branch of the Belle family."

"Perhaps you'd like to see some portraits?"

Her face lit up. "Pictures? The family albums?"

"Paintings. We aren't sure who some of them are, but maybe you'll recognize the faces and help us fill in the blanks."

"Um, well . . . sure."

"The paintings are in this room." She led them to a smaller storage area separate from the big room they were in. Charmaine followed her without enthusiasm.

Light fell through dormer windows. Jillian pulled dust sheets off the portraits, and she arranged them to face outward.

"Neither Bertie nor Aunt Cornelia knows who any of these people are," she said, "but we decided they were either long-ago in-laws or distant relatives. Do any of these faces or features ring a bell with you, Charmaine?"

The woman wore an expression of complete boredom until she caught Jillian studying her. She put on a bright smile and lifted her brows as though nothing could interest her more than the portraits of unknown relatives. She studied the images of each of the two women and three men who, judging by their apparel and hairstyle, spanned the decades from the 1890s to the 1930s.

"Sorry, honey lamb, but I don't see anything that looks familiar. Well, maybe that woman's weak chin resembles Great-Great-Great-Uncle Farbes's son's wife, but that's it."

"Farbes?"

"Yes. Maybe he wasn't an uncle, though. Maybe he was a cousin." She flipped one hand dismissively. "It's so hard to remember when one has so many ancestors, isn't it?" She scowled at the dog in her arms. "Dipsy Dee, my goodness, you're wriggling a lot. Bryce, I think this dog needs to go outside."

She turned to look for Bryce. Not seeing him, she walked out of the gallery. She glanced around, a deep frown slicing between her eyebrows. "Bryce!" She walked back into the gallery, yelled for him again, looking around.

"I don't see him," Jillian said. "But maybe he needed a little break. There are no bathrooms up here. He might be downstairs."

"He better hope he's downstairs, running off without a word to me when I need him."

Charmaine headed to the stairs and stomped down them, yelling for Bryce. In her grasp, the dog struggled and whined.

"Be quiet, you stupid dog!" she screeched. "Here. Take it." She shoved Dipsy Doodle into Jillian's hands and stormed along the second floor hallway. "Bryce, where are you?"

"Please don't yell," Jillian said. "You'll disturb Aunt Cornelia. And you're upsetting poor little Dipsy Doodle."

"I don't care. I'm upset enough for all of us!"

Cornelia emerged from her room, clutching the collar of her starched white blouse as if caught in a cold wind. "What on earth is going on?"

Charmaine pivoted sharply and faced her. "I'll tell you what's going on. That low-down, good-for-nothing Bryce Birmingham is nowhere to be found, *that's* what's going on. If he has walked out on me, you'd better believe he'll pay for it."

Birmingham? Jillian thought his last name was Bellingham.

Charmaine threw open the door to Bryce's room farther down the hallway, but he wasn't in there. She marched to the head of the staircase and yelled for him.

Trembling, her tense body hard as a rock, Dipsy Doodle alternated between yipping and howling. No amount of soft talk and gentle rubs could calm the dog in Jillian's arms.

"You're upsetting Dipsy Dee," Jillian said again, hoping to get through Charmaine's anger.

"That dog is not nearly as upset as I am." She clomped down the stairs.

Jillian followed with Cornelia behind her, clucking and muttering. Halfway down, Jillian paused and turned a concerned gaze to her great-aunt.

"Why don't you go back to your room? I'll sort this out."

Cornelia glanced at the softly yipping dog as though wondering if yipping was the right sound to make.

"I'll decide if and when I need to return to my room."

She descended the rest of the way, head high, thin back straight and stiff, aloof and queenly. She was quite a contrast to the plump, agitated Charmaine.

"There he is, that wretch!" Charmaine pointed out the back window in the living room.

Past the unkempt gardenia bushes and halfway across the rain-misted meadow behind Belle Haven, Bryce trudged toward the house. Charmaine threw open the door to the veranda and stepped out into the damp morning.

"What do you think you're doing? Where have you been? Why did you leave me?" She yelled each question at the highest volume, even as he passed the gardenias and stepped onto the veranda.

"The dust in the gallery bothered my allergies, so I stepped out for some fresh air before I became ill."

Charmaine planted her fists on both hips and glared at him, one foot tapping rapidly. "You stepped out for air without a word that you were going, without so much as a 'by your leave'?" Her honeyed accent had disappeared. "What if I needed you? What if there had been an emergency?"

"I only walked across the meadow as far as the trees and back. I've been gone less than ten minutes."

She continued to steam, her eyes narrowed, her face red. Bryce looked past her to Jillian, who stood in the open door, trying to comfort the whimpering dog. He brushed off any dampness from his clothes and stepped around Charmaine.

"You should try to calm down before your migraine returns—"

"You should have thought of that before you ran off. If my headache comes back, it'll be your fault."

"I'll take Dipsy Dee," he said.

The dog practically leaped from Jillian's grasp and into his arms. She buried her fuzzy face against his chest, fluffy tail wagging.

Bryce was his usual calm, collected self, as if Charmaine's tirade and rage were nothing.

Even so, when Jillian met his eyes she saw a banked fire burning in their depths. Something dark was ready to flare into action. One day Charmaine would push him too far.

After the tour earlier that day, and after Charmaine and Bryce had retreated to their separate rooms, Jillian nipped into her bedroom and locked the door. She didn't want an unexpected visit from Charmaine or Cornelia while she talked with her best friend. She called Savannah and, as briefly but as thoroughly as possible, shared her concerns about this new cousin.

"Honestly, Savannah, she's as fake as a seven-dollar bill. Her accent comes and goes, and I think she's picked up her 'Southern charm' by reading old novels. Have you ever heard anyone actually say 'oh, my stars and stripes' or 'Land *of* Goshen'?"

Savannah's clear laugh rang across the phone. "'Land o' Goshen,' yes. My granny used to say that, but what you're talking about sounds disingenuous."

"She's as mean as a snake to Bryce. And I think that poor little dog is afraid of her."

"That's terrible. Bryce seemed to treat the dog kindly when I saw them at the bakery, but do you think he's phony too?"

"It stands to reason that if Charmaine's a fake, so is he. But the thing is, he doesn't act the way she does. In fact, he barely reacts at all. If I were him, I'd leave her high and dry. I wonder if she's got something on him."

"You mean maybe she knows something about him, something secret?"

"Yes."

"But what could it be?"

Jillian scooted over on the bed until she rested her back against the headboard.

"I have no clue, but I'm telling you, Savannah, there is something fishy about these people. I looked up their names on the Internet and found nothing. And you should have heard the convoluted family history Charmaine gave us. I looked up Hoyt Belle online and went to the library to read what *The History of Moss Hollow* book had about him but learned nothing new. I found absolutely nothing about this alleged great-great-great-great-grandmother, whom Charmaine claims was the daughter of Hoyt Belle and his, once again alleged, third wife."

"That's a lot of greats. Did you tell Bertie and Cornelia?"

"Not yet." Jillian chewed on her lower lip. "In spite of the fact that the two of them allowed Charmaine and Bryce to stay at Belle Haven, they aren't exactly happy with these people being here, and until I can get more information, I don't want to upset them unnecessarily. Bertie is her usual hospitable, generous self, but I think Charmaine has frayed Aunt Cornelia's last nerve. I'd like to oust the pair from Belle Haven, but as long as there's the least bit of possibility that we're related, neither Bertie nor Aunt Cornelia will agree to that, no matter how much they want to."

"Yes, it would be like serving instant tea and canned biscuits, wouldn't it?"

"Almost that bad," Jillian said with a slight laugh. "So before the situation gets worse or before Charmaine does something unforgivable, I need to gather as much information as possible and formulate a plan."

"Have you thought about hiring a private investigator?"

"I'm considering it." She sat straight and leaned forward as if her friend sat on the bed with her. "Listen, Savannah. Would you help me?"

"You know I will. What do you want me to do?"

"To start with, come for dinner tonight."

"Oh, well, if you're going to use strong-arm tactics like that . . ."

Jillian gave a little laugh. "I mean, if you could come for dinner, hang around, and keep your eyes and ears open. Watch for anything that seems suspicious. Maybe you can worm a bit of information out of Bryce."

"What? You mean like Mata Hari?"

"Yes. Well, not exactly. Don't be seductive or sultry. Just be . . . available. For a chat, I mean. You don't have to flirt with him or lure him away with your feminine wiles or anything tacky. Not that Charmaine would let you, anyway. Please?"

"And shoulder some of the burden? Absolutely. Shall I come a little early?"

"Yes. Thank you, Savannah. You are a friend indeed."

Savannah Cantrell's calming presence at dinner that evening worked its magic. The six sat at the table, enjoying tall glasses of sweet tea, Cornelia's spicy gumbo, and Jillian's corn bread.

"Cousin Jilly," Charmaine said, grabbing another hunk of corn bread from the plate, "this is absolutely the best corn bread ever."

"She's right." Bertie picked up the old blue willow plate that held the golden wedges and passed it around. "Anyone else want more?"

"It practically melts in your mouth," Cornelia said, taking another piece.

Savannah cut a wedge in half and stared down at it. "I want more, but three and half servings are plenty." She patted her flat tummy. "So share your recipe, Jillian."

Bertie beamed at her, and Cornelia turned an expectant expression on her. Jillian's smile made her cheeks ache.

"No actual recipe other than Bertie's usual one," she said, "but I did play around with it a bit by adding some sour cream, some frozen corn from last year's harvest, a bit of cayenne pepper. And I baked it a tad longer than usual because I love the crust to be brown and crunchy."

"That can be tricky," Bertie said. "Bake it too long and you'll have a dry, tasteless mess, but you did a fantastic job on this, Jillian. I believe you have become the official corn bread baker of Belle Haven."

Everyone laughed, and the evening progressed far more smoothly than Jillian could have hoped. The talk was easy and friendly, as if the afternoon had not bristled in an atmosphere full of strain. Bryce and Charmaine were cordial to their hosts and to Savannah, but said nothing to each other.

Jillian was afraid that the pleasant tone of the evening would be short-lived. Bryce's interest was nearly palpable the moment Savannah stepped through the front door that evening. His aloof, stoic nature softened, and he hardly took his eyes off her. Jillian wasn't sure Savannah had noticed yet, but Charmaine had. Thus far, she'd said nothing about it, but the woman's need to be the center of his attention guaranteed a confrontation sooner or later. From what Jillian had come to expect with these two, she figured that Charmaine biding her time this way served a larger purpose for her. But Jillian had no idea what that purpose might be.

She also wondered how much abuse a personal assistant was expected to take before quitting the job. Had she been in Bryce's place, she would have walked out on the woman long ago. And seeing how ugly Charmaine could be to Dipsy Doodle, Jillian would have taken the dog with her.

Jillian was developing a growing affection for the little canine, realizing the poor thing felt uncertain and frightened most of the time she'd been at Belle Haven. The dog seemed to trust Jillian. At that moment, she was under the table, her tiny chin resting on Jillian's foot.

"Have you been enjoying your stay at Belle Haven?" Savannah asked Charmaine and Bryce brightly.

"It's been quite pleasant," Bryce said, offering her a small, hesitant smile.

Charmaine took one last bite of corn bread and hurriedly swallowed it before she turned to Savannah. A dab of butter clung to one corner of the woman's full pink lips.

"Oh, honey doll, yes, we've been having a marvelous time." She dabbed her mouth with a napkin. "Jillian insisted on taking us through this entire mansion today, all the way to the unused gallery upstairs. She said she'll take us all over the entire estate when the ground dries out. Even the root cellar out back."

Bertie and Cornelia drew their spines straight and threw identical disapproving looks at Jillian, mouths turned down, brows furrowed.

"I never said anything about—" she began, but the doorbell rang, interrupting her defense. All too gladly she escaped the dinner table to go to the door.

A man in dark slacks, a white shirt, and a jacket stood on the other side of the threshold. He ran one hand over his thinning brown hair. "Is this Belle Haven?" he asked.

"Yes, it is. May I help you?"

"I'm Jack Porter." He paused, as if waiting for her to recognize his name or react in some way. "I'm a friend of Charmaine's. I'd like to talk to her, please."

"Charmaine's friend?" Jillian didn't try to keep the surprise off her face or out of her voice. *I should have known Charmaine would invite friends to Belle Haven without a word to us.*

"Yes. She said she was coming down here."

Apparently, the man's strong voice carried into the dining room. Conversation at the table suddenly fell silent.

"*Jack?*" Charmaine shrieked. "Jack Porter! What are *you* doing here?"

Chair legs scraped loudly against the floor, and she rushed to the door, pushing Jillian to one side. Dipsy Doodle followed, barking madly. A cab waited in the light rain. Jack Porter turned and waved it on.

"How dare you follow me here?" Charmaine yelled, glaring at him. She pointed at the disappearing taillights. "And you better run after that taxicab because you're going to need a ride right back to where you came from."

The others had gathered in the large doorway between the dining room and foyer. Cornelia gaped at the newcomer. Jillian tensed and reached into the pocket of her slacks for her cell phone in case this newest development turned into something worse. Bryce scooped up Dipsy Doodle and calmed her with his quiet words.

"What's going on?" Bertie asked.

Jillian tipped her head toward the couple at the front door. "I'm not quite sure."

Charmaine thrust her head outside and looked around as if checking for more unexpected visitors. Her face was red with rage as she turned to Jack.

"You think I want everyone in the state of Georgia seeing you follow me around like a mangy hound? Get in here!" Charmaine yanked the fellow across the threshold and slammed the door.

"I'm not making a scene, Charmie," he said.

"Do *not* call me Charmie! How many times have I told you I hate it?"

He blushed, but he didn't back down. "Charmaine, we have to get this thing settled between us."

"Oh, for heaven's sake." She turned from him impatiently and started to stalk away but pivoted to face him again. "Have you no shame, no pride? Can't you get it through your thick head that there is nothing left to settle?"

This was a personal matter that neither party seemed inclined to keep private, and it was likely to go on for a while. Doubting she needed to call law enforcement, Jillian put away her cell phone. She turned to the others, and with a slight dip of her head, she subtly beckoned them to follow her into the library, away from Jack and Charmaine. She turned on the green-shaded desk lamp atop a cherry wood desk and the three Tiffany lamps on various small tables, giving the room an intimate, cozy, old-fashioned glow.

"What's going on?" Cornelia asked. "Who's that man?"

Everyone looked at Bryce, who stood near the open library doors and maintained every appearance of straining to hear the conversation in the foyer. Rubbing Dipsy Doodle's head gently, he took a couple of steps farther into the library.

"They recently broke up," he murmured. "That is, Charmaine broke off their engagement, and Jack isn't happy about it."

"Ooh," the sisters said, almost in unison.

"Then, obviously, their conversation is nothing we need to be a party to." Jillian firmly closed the library's double doors, though she would have loved to press her ear against the door panel and eavesdrop.

Savannah tucked one hand in the crook of Bryce's arm and led him to a leather settee near the fireplace. "Dipsy Doodle is so cute and such a sweet little thing," she said. "Is she still a puppy?"

"No. She's three years old."

Savannah petted the dog's head and received a quick, polite lick on the hand in return. "She is *so* cute."

"Thank you," Bryce said, smiling. "She's a nice little lapdog. And she knows a few tricks. Watch." He set Dipsy Doodle on the floor and gave the usual series of commands.

With each "sit," "stay," and "roll over" that Bryce spoke, Savannah softly clapped her hands and exclaimed, "What a good girl!"

Jillian had not seen Bryce's face as relaxed or his eyes as lively as they were right then. She almost hated that she'd asked Savannah to draw him out. It seemed so sneaky and underhanded.

But I have Bertie's and Aunt Cornelia's welfares to consider. I have to make sure no one takes advantage of their good natures.

The fireplace had been converted to gas three or four decades ago but was rarely used. Always closed off, the room tended to gather gloom and chill around it like a second skin, especially with rain pattering at the windows. Jillian turned on the gas flame and adjusted the thermostat. The scorched, dusty smell soon burned away as the fire added some cheeriness to the room. It did nothing, though, to take away the worried expressions from her grandmother's and great-aunt's faces.

"Bertie," Jillian said, groping for something, anything, to redirect their attention, "don't you think we should go through these books at some point? They need to be dusted and aired. We have some old volumes here that undoubtedly would be better off in the care of the historical society or kept in the rare books collection at the library."

Although he was happily engaged in conversation with Savannah near the fireplace, Bryce had heard what she said.

"With your kind permission, I'd like to look at these old books while I'm here," he said.

Bertie turned to him. "Are you a collector?"

"Not really, but I do love them."

"We are not getting rid of any of them," Cornelia said firmly. "The family has collected them over the years, so why should we blithely toss them aside?" She waved one hand as if flinging something away.

"But, Aunt Cornelia, we aren't reading them. They aren't even organized. Look." She tapped the dark leather spine of one book and the bright-blue spine of the one next to it. "Charles Dickens next to Jackie Collins. Which ancestor bought Jackie Collins?"

Savannah giggled, but Cornelia sputtered and scowled. "I'll have you know that's a signed copy. I bought it in Atlanta and stood right there as she signed it. And I already told you I will organize these books one of these days."

Jillian let a few seconds pass before trying a different tack. "Charmaine asked earlier if we had any family history books. We don't, do we?"

Cornelia sniffed as if the idea insulted her and held her silence.

"I don't think we do," Bertie said. "If there is anything of note that was not given to the historical society long ago, it has been tucked away in some obscure place and totally forgotten."

"That's right." Cornelia's frosty gaze settled on a spot in the middle of the air.

"Honestly, though, this is such a lovely library," Savannah said. "If it was sparkling clean and organized, it would be such a fabulous asset to Belle Haven."

Bryce sat forward, leaning toward the others.

"Let me do some work in here." The enthusiasm with which he made this offer surprised everyone. "I studied library science in college, so I have some knowledge." He ran his gaze over the entire collection, taking in two stories of bulging bookshelves.

Jillian followed his gaze. "But there's so much dust. On everything."

Bryce met her eyes. "I don't mind. I'll get some over-the-counter allergy pills at the pharmacy in town. In fact, much of the dust in here is from the deterioration of the books themselves. And that wonderful old book smell? I love it."

He inhaled deeply, and the others did the same. It was the fragrance of libraries and used bookstores.

"If Charmaine doesn't object," he continued, "I'd like to do it. Frankly, I crave some variety in my days."

"But will you be here that long?" Savannah asked.

He looked down at Dipsy Doodle and rubbed her ears. "I don't know how long Charmaine plans to stay. It's totally up to her—and you, of course." He lifted his head and glanced at Savannah, then Jillian. "But whether it's a day or a week or a month, I'd cherish the opportunity to work in this library."

"That's a really great suggestion, Bryce, and a generous offer," Savannah said, smiling at him. She glanced at the others. "Isn't it?"

But that means they might stay here even longer, Jillian thought. *Weeks, maybe even months.*

Savannah met Jillian's gaze and looked away quickly, blushing. What did that mean? Was her friend developing a genuine interest in Bryce? That was not exactly what Jillian had in mind when she had asked Savannah for help.

"We couldn't ask you to do that," Bertie said. Jillian figured her grandmother envisioned unreasonable demands and temper tantrums.

"You didn't ask. I offered."

"Guests do not work at Belle Haven." Cornelia's prim tone said she did not want his help in that library, ever.

He stared at her a moment, then passed a gaze over the others and sat back. The eager light died in his eyes. "I see." He gathered up Dipsy Doodle and held her close, retreating into his usual silence.

Savannah shot a look at Jillian.

Jillian cleared her throat. "I have an idea."

"You would," Cornelia sniped grimly. "You always do."

Jillian ignored her. "How about if you go through the books on just a few of the shelves, Bryce? Perhaps you can give Aunt Cornelia and me some suggestions how to organize the rest of them. That wouldn't be work. Not exactly, would it?"

Everyone turned to Cornelia. Surely her great-aunt would see the banked hope in the man's eyes.

"Cornelia, think about it." Savannah's bright smile shone on the elderly woman. "A trained, educated person to help you get started is a fabulous idea."

Cornelia chewed thoughtfully on her lower lip, but Bertie had no hesitation. "I agree. Let the boy work on these books, for goodness' sake. You've complained about the state of the library often enough. Don't look a gift horse in the mouth." A sudden expression crossed her face, and she hurriedly added, "Not that we think of you as a gift horse, Bryce."

"Of course not," Jillian said.

"No, indeed," Savannah chimed in.

"Well, now, I—"

The library doors flew open, and Charmaine marched in with her hands covering her ears. "I'm not listening to you, Jack. Not a word."

"But, darlin'," he said, "you don't understand."

"Where's Dipsy Dee?" she shouted as if to drown out his wheedling voice. "Give her to me." She sailed toward Bryce and roughly took the dog from him. "Hush!" she said when Dipsy Doodle yipped. "Bryce, you come with Dipsy Dee and me. Jack, I don't care where you go, but do not come anywhere near me again. Ever. Bryce, come. *Now!*"

Without waiting for him, she stalked out of the room, the whimpering dog in her grip. Bryce hurried out after her, leaving the others to deal with Jack Porter.

Jack watched Charmaine and Bryce go, his face turning hard and dark, hands curling into fists. Savannah and Jillian exchanged glances.

"Did you ever?" Cornelia fiddled with her necklace and stared at the newcomer, her expression a mask of confusion and worry.

"I'll fix us some tea," Bertie said into the uncomfortable silence that followed.

"Yes, do." Cornelia's tone held a slight measure of relief. "There's nothing that settles a body's nerves better on a stormy night than a cup of tea. I'll help you, Sister." The two of them bustled out, their blonde-gray heads tipped toward each other, talking in worried undertones.

Thunder rumbled, vibrating the old mansion's floors and rattling the windows. Savannah crossed to one of the windows and pulled back the edge of a faded velvet drapery. As she peeked outside, lightning flared, silhouetting her against the coming storm. The lights flickered. "The weather forecast said we were in for another round of bad weather. Looks like it's already gearing up." She let the curtain fall into place and turned from the window.

"You should go before it starts, Savannah." Jillian tried to keep the reluctance out of her voice. Her friend was like a soothing balm on a stinging wound. "Driving in these spring storms can be treacherous."

"Yes, they can be, but if you need me to stay longer, I will."

"I want you to be safe," Jillian reassured her. "Maybe we can have lunch tomorrow, if the weather breaks."

"*If* the weather breaks." Savannah turned to Jack Porter. "May I give you a lift back into town, Mr. Porter?"

He offered her a weak smile but shook his head. "No, ma'am. I'm not leaving unless Charmie comes with me."

No more unexpected, unwelcome overnight visitors in our home! Jillian screamed silently. *Especially if they are going to quarrel with each other.*

"I doubt she'll come downstairs again tonight," she told him. "I've only known her for two days, but it's perfectly clear she's determined to have her way."

And that's a Belle family trait for sure.

"She is muleheaded, but I'm as stubborn as she is, and I'm not leaving until I get what I came for." He cleared his throat. "I don't mean to be uncouth, ma'am, but you have a nice, big place here, and I'd be grateful if you could put me up for the night."

We are two guest towels away from running a free bed-and-breakfast.

There was no guarantee the man wouldn't go to Charmaine's room and harass her, or that Charmaine wouldn't come after him, claws unsheathed. These people were little more than strangers to Jillian, and she had no idea what to expect. What if one of them pulled a knife or a gun?

"Mr. Porter, I hate to be ungracious, but I refuse to have the peace of our home disturbed. I will not allow you and Charmaine to upset my grandmother and great-aunt."

His face turned bright red, and he ducked his head.

"Yes, ma'am. I understand. I'm so sorry about earlier. Charmie doesn't like surprises. I should have planned better." He lifted his head. "But I promise, if you'll put me up for the night, it will all be taken care of tomorrow morning. If not, I'll leave before noon anyway. You have my word on it."

"What does that mean, 'it will all be taken care of'?"

"Just that if we give her a chance to get some sleep and get over the surprise of seeing me, she'll be all right. She's thrown me out before and called me back before I got to the car. Trust me, ma'am. She's in a snit, but she'll get over it. She always does."

Her grandmother had taught her long ago to be kind and caring, hospitable to those in need, but enough was enough.

"I'm sorry, Mr. Porter. As I said, I have an obligation of looking out for my family and our home. After the antics I witnessed tonight, I must insist you leave."

The look he gave her was one of near powerlessness.

"But I promise—"

"I'm sorry." She glanced at Savannah, pleading for backup.

"Moss Hollow has a charming, comfortable hotel nearby, Mr. Porter," Savannah said. "The rates are very reasonable. They offer guests a fresh slice of peach pie any time, day or night, and believe me when I say they are known for that peach pie. Besides, you seem like a gentleman. I'm sure you don't want to upset our elderly hostesses, do you?"

"I . . . well, of course I don't want to upset folks. That's not why I'm here. I only want to set things straight with Charmaine.

"You can do that tomorrow," Jillian said.

"Of course you can." Savannah smiled warmly, taking his arm as if being escorted to dinner. "I might even be persuaded to have a slice of that pie with you."

He gaped at her, then blushed. "Well . . . all right then."

At the door, Savannah turned around and sent Jillian a silent message. She was pretty sure that message was *You owe me one.*

By two a.m. Wednesday, Jillian had been staring up at the ceiling of her bedroom for three hours. She had flipped and fluffed her pillow at least twenty times, and twice she got out of bed to smooth her sheets and adjust the light blanket. Frequent lightning flashes and nearly ceaseless rumbles and growls of thunder drew her away from any sleep she might have encountered. In a lull, she heard a bedroom door open and someone pad down the hallway. Charmaine had probably wakened Bryce to send him downstairs to fetch her a sandwich or a piece of pie. She was that kind of woman.

It wasn't just the storm that kept Jillian awake. The thought of Jack Porter also chased away sleep. When Savannah hadn't called or texted by eleven o'clock that night, Jillian sent her a text, thanking her for taking Jack away and asking if everything went all right. The reply had been Savannah's typical, no-nonsense texting: *No probs, no peach pie. Dropped him off, went home. Talk 2 u later.*

Was Jack stalking Charmaine? To follow someone all the way from Virginia to Georgia was either devotion or obsession. Either way, it was too much. What would happen when he returned this morning, as promised? What did he have planned? Jillian would have to be on her toes. *What if things get physical?* She shuddered and then tried to push troublesome thoughts from her mind so she could rest. But, with plenty of thunder, lightning, and pounding rain, the storm did its best to prevent her from going to sleep.

At some point, she heard Dipsy Doodle barking. By then, the storm had moved on, and the rain had finally stopped. She hoped Charmaine or Bryce would take the dog out to relieve itself soon.

Bryce said she never messed in the house. Jillian hoped he was right, because all the wooden floors had been refinished not long ago. Plus, there were new rugs everywhere.

She pulled a pillow over her head to mute the barks and slipped back into sleep. When she woke again, a glance at her phone showed the time was four thirty. As worn out as they were from the last few days, Bertie and Cornelia would soon be stirring. Jillian refused to lie in bed when she should be up helping them.

She took a quick shower and got dressed. By the time she went downstairs, daylight had begun to seep sluggishly through the stained glass dome. If the day was clear, the light shining down from the skylight would bathe the foyer in golden light. Jillian looked forward to seeing it after so many days of gloomy weather.

Belle Haven was so quiet, Jillian knew she was the only one up and around.

Thank goodness the storm is over. I hope we've seen the last of the rain for a while.

She flipped on the kitchen light and was rewarded with sorrowful, high-pitched howling. She froze, listening hard. The sound came from outside.

"Surely that isn't Dipsy Dee," she said aloud, hurriedly crossing to the windows. She pulled back the curtains. There on the veranda sat the little white dog, soaking wet, shivering, staring at Jillian through misery-filled eyes.

"Oh my goodness."

Jillian flung open the door and picked up the sodden, trembling scrap of fur. Dipsy Doodle snuggled herself as close to Jillian as she could, as if trying to bury herself in her warmth. Muddy paw prints were thick along the bottom windows and door where the dog had scratched, begging for entrance.

"Oh, you poor little thing. Bless your little heart."

Inside, Jillian grabbed a thick towel from the mudroom and wrapped the dog in it. She cuddled Dipsy Doodle close, murmuring and crooning, ignoring the dirty tracks all over her white shirt.

"I'm so sorry, Dipsy Dee," she said, looking into the little black eyes. "I should have gotten up and checked when I heard you barking. I had no idea you were outside. Poor, poor little thing."

She dried the soppy fur as gently and thoroughly as possible, then took two more towels from the mudroom and fashioned them into a soft, dry bed for Dipsy Doodle. She placed it in the kitchen corner nearest the stove and tenderly settled the dog on it. Still shivering, but no longer whimpering, Dipsy Doodle curled in on herself, lowered her head, and closed her eyes.

Jillian had never spent a lot of time around animals, but she knew leaving a small dog, pampered or not, out in a chilly rain was just plain wrong. She filled a bowl with water and loosely scrambled an egg, but Dipsy Doodle ignored the offerings, as if food and water were too little, too late.

"Goodness me!" Bertie bustled into the kitchen, adjusting her blouse and tightening her belt. "I'll never again take another pill to help me sleep, even if it's herbal. A good rainstorm should be enough." She glanced at the clock on the kitchen stove. "Look what time it is. Why didn't you get me up? Have you made coffee? And why are you sitting over there on the floor?"

"You needed that extra sleep, Bertie. And no, I haven't made the coffee yet, but I will in a minute." Jillian expelled a long breath. "I'm on the floor because . . . well, look." She pointed at Dipsy Doodle.

Bertie looked. A frown deepened her wrinkles as she approached.

"Is that Charmaine's dog? Why is it in here? Dogs should not be in the kitchen."

Jillian was hardly able to speak around the knot in her throat. "I know, but—" Her voice broke and she swallowed hard. "Dipsy Doodle has been out in the rain most of the night. She needs to be where it's warm and dry."

"She what?" Bertie bent to get a closer look. "All night? Why, I wonder why she didn't bark to be let in."

"She did. I heard her, but I didn't know she was outside. I thought she was just kicking up a fuss, and now I feel awful that I didn't get up and check on her."

Bertie shook her head and straightened. "I didn't hear a thing. As if oversleeping on a Wednesday morning wasn't bad enough, not hearing a helpless creature needing help . . . Oh, I'm going to flush those pills right down the drain." She eyed the dog again. "She hasn't moved. Is she . . . all right?"

Jillian placed a hand on Dipsy Doodle's side; she felt her rhythmic breathing. "She's alive, if that's what you mean."

"But why on earth was she outside? The way those two dote on that dog, I hardly see how they could let her stay out overnight."

Jillian stroked the small head. "Actually, Charmaine does not dote. I think Dipsy Doodle is more of an accessory to her than a pet. Bryce seems to care for the poor little thing, though, and I'm surprised he let this happen."

"Then he wouldn't have left the dog outside."

"No, and since his bedroom faces the other side of the house, he probably did not hear her barking. I doubt Charmaine would have bothered to get up and take her out, no matter how badly Dipsy Dee needed to go. She probably wasn't even downstairs."

Bertie twisted her mouth in thought. "Well then, the dog must have gotten outside some other way. But how?"

Jillian studied Dipsy Doodle, watching the furry sides rise and fall regularly. A thought crept into her mind. A horrible thought that left guilt in its wake, and she was almost too ashamed to acknowledge it. She pushed herself off the floor and spoke in a low tone.

"Bertie, I hate to think this, but you know how Aunt Cornelia fussed and complained about Dipsy Doodle, and how she's afraid the dog is going to eat Possum or something? Do you think . . . I mean, it's not likely she would have, well, you know . . ." She jerked her head toward the window, where a faint golden sunrise was chasing gray from the sky. "You don't think she would've put the dog outside, do you?"

Bertie's mouth flew open. "Jillian Amanda Green, you hush that kind of talk right now. Your great-aunt would no more turn a dog out on a rainy night than skinny-dip in the Robert E. Lee Memorial Fountain over in Tosco."

"But if Aunt Cornelia didn't turn out the dog, who did?"

As if their words had summoned her, Cornelia came into the kitchen looking bright and well rested. Possum padded along, a couple of steps behind her. "Why are you two over here whispering in the corner like schoolgirls telling secrets?"

Her sharp gaze fell on Dipsy Doodle. She stopped so suddenly that the cat walked into her.

"What is that thing doing in our kitchen?" She glowered and pointed. "Possum will have a literal hissy fit."

But, much to their astonishment, Possum seemed to have developed a change of heart. Rather than arching his back and fluffing out his cream-colored fur in a show of dominance, the cat approached Dipsy Doodle slowly, silently, carefully. With the bare tip of his pink nose, he touched the furry white head, then gently sniffed the dog's entire length. He paused, looked over his shoulder to give the three women a soulful gaze, then turned and licked one canine ear.

Dipsy Doodle opened her eyes and hesitantly wagged her tail a couple of times. Possum snuggled close, and the dog lowered her head once more.

"Why, did you ever?" Cornelia said.

The women watched, marveling at the newly discovered companionship.

Jillian turned to Cornelia. "Aunt Cornelia," she said as gently as she could, "someone put Dipsy Doodle outside during the night. Do you know who it was?"

Cornelia looked at Jillian as if she had spoken Japanese. "How on earth would I know?"

"Dipsy Dee is a sweet little dog who's afraid of being in a new place and around a lot of strange people. Look at her. She craves attention and affection like any other dog."

"That may be, but why is she in the kitchen instead of with our guests, where she belongs?"

"That's what I'm telling you," Jillian said. "When I came downstairs this morning, she was sitting out there on the veranda, looking half-drowned. Someone obviously put her out in the rain sometime in the middle of the night and left her there."

Cornelia's face changed, taking on a soft, tender expression as she looked at the dog. "Why, that poor little thing! Who'd do something like . . . Wait a minute." She turned a hurt look on Jillian. "You thought *I* had put her out into that weather?"

"Well, to be honest, Cornelia, you have been terribly cranky about Dipsy," Bertie reminded her. "And Jillian didn't say you *did*. She asked if you *had*."

"It's all the same. If she thought it, she believed it." Cornelia lifted her chin and sailed across the room to make coffee.

"Aunt Cornelia, please. I didn't mean anything."

"If you don't mean anything, you shouldn't say anything."

Jillian glanced at her grandmother, who rolled her eyes and got her car keys from the peg next to the back door. "I'm going to the bakery. Poor Lenora is probably up to her eyebrows in bread dough." She hesitated, then asked, "Can you manage our guests, Cornelia, or shall Jillian stay here again today?"

Cornelia waved her away without looking at her. "I have been known to take care of myself and others before. Without help from *anyone*."

"I'll call to check on things when I have a minute later on." Bertie looked at Jillian. "Go ahead and help with breakfast here first. And change your shirt, dear. You have muddy paw prints all over it."

Cornelia shrugged, but Jillian nodded. "It's okay, Bertie. We'll be fine."

Even after her sister was gone, Cornelia wore hurt feelings like a mink stole. With her lips pressed firmly together as if she'd never speak again, she took a carton of eggs, a block of cheese, and a container of assorted chopped vegetables from the refrigerator.

Bryce came into the kitchen, his royal-blue dressing gown neatly tied at the waist and his sleek brown hair combed.

"Good morning," Jillian said. "Help yourself to coffee, and we'll have breakfast made soon. Did you sleep well?"

"I did, thank you." He glanced around as if seeking something.

"She's right there in the corner," Jillian said, "though how she got outside is a mystery. I'm sure you didn't put her out in the rain." She took plates from the cabinet.

"I beg your pardon?"

"Dipsy Doodle. I brought her in and dried her off."

"Dipsy Dee?" His gaze landed on the dog and cat in the corner. "My word! She was outside?"

Jillian stared at him. "You mean you didn't miss her?"

He hurried across the room, scooped up Dipsy Doodle, and held her close, burying his face in her furry side for a moment. "She always sleeps with Charmaine. Was she out very long?"

"I'd say for quite a while. She was soaked through and very cold."

"I don't understand . . ." He looked her over carefully. "She's lethargic, but she seems all right."

"Maybe she needs to sleep," Cornelia said.

"After breakfast, you might want to take her to Dr. Shane West," Jillian said. "He's Possum's veterinarian and is very good."

"I'll do that, thank you." Bryce settled Dipsy Doodle onto her bed again and hunkered on the floor beside her, murmuring quietly.

"Possum has been looking after your dog, bless his heart," Cornelia added as if Possum was the designated animal sitter for all of Nathan County.

"Why, thank you, Possum," he said, giving the cat's chin a gentle scratch.

"Possum says, 'You're welcome.' Jillian, slice the bread for toast, please. I'll have these eggs finished in a flash."

Bryce stroked Possum's soft fur, smiling at him.

"Has Charmaine been down to check on Dipsy Dee?" he asked.

"Not yet," Jillian replied. "Maybe her headache came back."

Cornelia guided her whisk through the eggs in the cast-iron skillet, then added the fresh vegetables. "Jillian, don't forget to set out the honey. Or would you rather have sorghum?" She looked at Bryce.

He blinked as if he had no idea what she meant. "Anything is fine, thank you."

The front door bell rang.

"Who could that be at this hour?" Cornelia said, looking at the kitchen clock and frowning.

For the second time in twenty-four hours, Jillian opened the door to Jack Porter.

Jack Porter gave Jillian a hesitant smile and ran his fingers through his thinning hair. His clothes were rumpled, and she realized they were the same clothes he'd worn the night before. He must have slept in them.

"I hope I'm not too early," he said. "I'm leaving soon and taking Charmaine with me, I hope. That's my rental." He jerked a thumb at a black economy car parked in the drive behind him.

"It's barely seven," she said.

"I know, but I couldn't sleep and decided to come on out. I've been sitting in the car for an hour."

"An hour?"

He nodded. "I could use some coffee, if you could spare a cup."

Jillian could hardly leave him on the doorstep, though she was sorely tempted.

"Sure. Come inside. We're about to have breakfast, and you may join us." She led him into the kitchen. "Aunt Cornelia and Bryce, Jack's here."

Cornelia's greeting was polite but subdued. The two men exchanged sour looks and said nothing to each other. Jillian understood. Last night was a fresh memory for everyone, and she didn't want a repeat. She invited them to sit at the breakfast table as she put down a plate of buttery toast, a jar of locally harvested honey, and a jar of dark-amber molasses. She filled coffee cups for them both and placed glasses of orange juice at each plate.

Jack spotted Dipsy Doodle and went to her. She raised her head a little and wagged her tail once, then retreated inside herself again.

"What happened to this poor little mutt?"

Jillian explained, and he shook his head. "I think some quiet rest and then some food and water will restore her."

"I wonder if Charmaine will be down soon," Cornelia said as she set down a large blue bowl of fluffy eggs scrambled with cheese, onions, and peppers. "I prefer to serve my guests food that is fresh and warm. Breakfast is ready, Mr. Porter. Come to the table."

With one final caress for Dipsy Doodle, Jack left her. "The food looks good, Miss Cornelia. Thank you." He sat down and pulled his chair closer to the table. "Charmie probably had trouble falling asleep."

"It's early for Charmaine to be up and about." Bryce pinned him with a glare. "If she had trouble sleeping, it was undoubtedly because you showed up without warning last night."

"Let's not start all that again," Jillian said. "I'm sure the storm caused enough noise and light to keep Rip Van Winkle awake all night," she added. "It certainly did me."

Cornelia settled at the table, asked the blessing, and passed the eggs.

"Maybe I should fix a tray and take it up to Charmaine," Jillian said, looking at her great-aunt.

Bryce scraped back his chair. "I'll do it."

Jack stood. "I can do it."

"It's my job." Bryce got to his feet. "I'm her personal assistant while you're little more than a castoff."

"A castoff!" Jack leaned forward. "Why you pompous little pantywaist. I ought to—"

"*Stop it!*" Jillian shrieked. "Sit down right now." She glared at them both until they sat. "Belle Haven is *our home*, not a reality show, and as one of Charmaine's . . . cousins, *I'll* do it."

All three at the table gaped at her. She supposed had she been in their shoes, she would have gawked too. Raising her voice and issuing commands was out of character. Right then, though, it also felt empowering.

"I declare, Jillian," Cornelia said. "Don't get your blood in an uproar."

"Sorry, Aunt Cornelia, but I refuse to have a repeat of last night's drama. Belle Haven is not Madison Square Garden."

"But a lady does not yell at the table."

"It was my fault. I apologize," Bryce said.

"Yeah, me too." Jack stared hungrily at the eggs and toast.

"Please have your own breakfast first," Bryce said to Jillian. "Charmaine probably isn't even up yet. I didn't hear her moving around when I went past her room, so she's probably still in bed, if not asleep. She'll let me know when she's ready to eat. She always does." His smile came and went so fast, Jillian wasn't sure she had even seen one. "If you want to prepare a tray, I will take it up to her." Bryce gave Jack a hard look. "That's my job."

Breakfast passed without further drama and in near silence, but tension hung around them like thick fog. Jillian wanted to escape the stressful atmosphere and settle her mind before going to The Chocolate Shoppe.

"It's such a beautiful morning, I'm going to step outside for a bit," Jillian said. "I'll clean the kitchen in a few minutes."

Cornelia followed Jillian onto the veranda. The morning air was filled with sweet fragrance and birdsong, but it was as humid as bathwater.

"Honey," Cornelia said, "do you think those two men are going to indulge in fisticuffs right here in Belle Haven?" Her eyes were troubled.

"They'd better not. I won't hesitate to call the police if they do, so don't fret."

"I'm not fretting, exactly."

"But you're worried."

"Yes. Something about those people . . ." She shook her head. "I'm sorry I fussed at you earlier."

"I understand, Aunt Cornelia. Having quarrelsome, pushy people in our home has upset us all. But please try not to worry. I doubt they'll be here much longer. I'm sorry if I hurt your feelings earlier. I know you'd never purposely do anything to hurt an animal. I was trying to sort out how and why Dipsy Doodle got outside."

"Ask that woman." She leaned closer to Jillian, tapped her temple, whispering. "She seems a little light in good sense. 'Airhead,' I think, is the term nowadays."

"I plan to ask her when I see her, believe me." In fact, she planned to do more than ask about the dog.

"See that you do." Cornelia made a dismissive gesture, as if trying to shake off all thoughts of unwanted cousins and their satellites. "And now, let's look at this back garden. I hope I have some blooms left after so much rain." She inhaled deeply. "Oh, I love the scent of gardenias in the morning. If we have enough, let's cut a bouquet to put in the living room, shall we? Another thing. I noticed a couple of dead limbs on that dogwood tree near the koi pond. You know, we really should get that pond cleaned out and restocked. It looks dreadful." She paused at the top step of the veranda to look back at Jillian. "Coming?"

Right then, Cornelia seemed so normal, it was as if the guests no longer bothered her. But Jillian knew her great-aunt was hiding thoughts and anxieties behind a genteel facade. Jillian did her best to act as if their world hadn't been tipped sideways.

"Yes, but just for a few minutes. I really need to help Bertie," Jillian said as they descended the steps. "She's worn out."

Cornelia flapped one hand. "My sister eats, lives, and breathes that bakery. She'll be all right a bit longer."

"Maybe so, but I don't like her being so overworked."

Cornelia stepped onto the ground and turned to frown at her great-niece. "Well, neither do I, if that's what you're thinking, but life at Belle Haven has gone off-kilter. I must maintain some kind of order here."

Jillian laid her hand on Cornelia's arm. "I know," she said softly.

Tears welled in the eighty-year-old's blue eyes, and Jillian's heart ached. Cornelia clutched her hand with chilly, unsteady fingers. "I don't like seeing our home unsettled."

"Neither do I, Aunt Cornelia. And I'm . . . well, let's say I'm looking into a few things."

"You are? What does that mean?"

"I'm taking care of Belle Haven, just the way you and Bertie have all these years. And I do not want you to worry. Promise?"

Cornelia studied her face as if she could unearth long-buried secrets. Finally, her expression relaxed. "All right. You were raised right, so I trust you to use that good raising and the sense the good Lord gave you."

Jillian leaned over and kissed the soft cheek. "I have been, and I'll continue to do so."

"Good. And it's the right thing to do, you helping your grandmother at the bakery. She's not as young as she used to be. But help me first for a few minutes. I want to get that bouquet." She took Jillian's arm in a firm clasp. "After the rain, everything is slippery, especially near the shed where my snippers and garden scissors are. That brick pathway is so old and broken down that it's dangerous. I shan't break a hip if I can help it. If that were to happen, I'd be no good to anyone."

Jillian had vowed to allow her great-aunt and her grandmother to feel and own as much independence and strength as possible for as long as possible. The last thing she wanted was for either of the two old dears to feel old or fragile, or, heaven forbid, *useless.*

"Just hang on to me, and we'll be careful where we step."

The mud was thick and red, as only Georgia mud can be. A bit of that on their clothes or shoes, and the stain would be there forever. They walked slowly, staying on the narrow brick walkway, watching their steps as they navigated around the saturated, mucky soil.

Jillian's grandfather had built the garden shed many years ago. With its steep roof and multipaned windows on either side of the door, the small building looked as if it belonged in a children's fairy tale.

"I haven't been inside that old shed for ages," Jillian said as they approached it. "What fun I used to have, playing in there."

"Oh, playing with your dolls and having pretend tea parties?"

Jillian laughed. "You know better than that. I've never been much of a girlie girl. Instead of a tea party, I was usually on some make-believe adventure, like being the first woman settler on the Alaskan frontier and this was my cabin. Or I pretended that I'd crash-landed on a remote planet and this was my shelter." She smiled as those memories returned.

"Mercy me. What an imagination."

"I know, but I had fun."

A toolbox had been built in beneath the window on the tiny porch. Cornelia opened it and frowned at the contents. She rummaged a bit, extracted a small pair of green-handled snips, and put them in her apron pocket.

"My scissors aren't here."

Jillian glanced inside it. "Where else might they be?"

Cornelia frowned. "Well, I don't know. I had them very recently. I realize I've been a little forgetful and distracted lately, but . . . what could I have done with them?" She looked around, squinting at the porch and the bushes growing around the shed. "Maybe there's another pair inside." She pulled a key ring from her pocket and fiddled with it, looking for the right key.

"Why do you keep the shed padlocked? No one but us even knows there's a shed back here."

She paused to give Jillian a look. "My dear, it's the law of averages. If you have items fit to be stolen, someone is going to come along and try to steal them. I'm sure that's written down in a book somewhere."

Jillian bit her lip to keep from giggling and watched her aunt unlock the shed door.

"Ah, finally, it opens. If you buy this brand of padlock, your belongings will be safe and sound. " Cornelia stepped inside. "I'm glad we have this one because I don't trust Charmaine and that boy."

"I know you don't." Jillian stood just outside the open door.

Cornelia looked over her shoulder. "I appreciate that their dog has come to an understanding with Possum, but I still believe there is something off about our guests. I'm about half-convinced that Charmaine is not kinfolk at all."

Not wanting to underscore her great-aunt's concerns, Jillian kept her opinions to herself. Her firm wish was that the visiting cousin and her entourage would soon depart Moss Hollow. In fact, as soon as she could come up with a workable plan to edge them back toward Virginia, she would implement it.

She stepped back as Cornelia came out of the shed with the garden scissors and locked the door. She was scowling as they descended the two steps off the porch.

"You know the one thing that is neither in the shed nor the toolbox?"

"A sledge hammer?"

"Oh, be serious. I can't lift a sledge hammer, let alone use one. I'm talking about gardening gloves. There are none in there. I refuse to work outside without gloves. The sun does such frightful things to our hands." She stretched out thin, well-kept hands and eyed them critically.

"I'll get you a pair in town today after we close the bakery."

"Don't bother. I'm sure I have a pair in the mudroom. Come along, dear." Again, she gripped Jillian's hand, and they picked their way across the broken walkway. "What a lovely morning, after all the rain. I'm so happy to see the sun again that I—" She stopped so abruptly that Jillian stumbled. "Jillian! What's that?" She pointed toward something nearly hidden in the gardenia bushes a few yards away.

Jillian narrowed her eyes against the light, trying to see. Sunlight streamed from the east. It sparkled on the wet grass and broadcast its brilliance over everything. Her vision adjusted, and her heart flopped.

"Oh my goodness! Aunt Cornelia, stand right here and don't move."

"Why? What is it?" Cornelia trotted behind her as Jillian rushed across the garden.

Inside the branches of a gardenia bush, completely rain-soaked, Charmaine Rawlins lay, curled as a comma. Jillian's long-lost cousin was dead!

12

Jillian did her best to shield her great-aunt from the grisly sight, but Cornelia struggled past her and saw the corpse.

"Who is that?" she shrieked, throwing out both arms wildly as if waving for help. "Is it Bertie?"

"No, Aunt Cornelia. It's Charmaine. You need to come away." Jillian grabbed the thin upper arms, but the screeching Cornelia lunged toward the dead woman.

"Get out of the way. I have to be sure it's not my sister lying there."

"Stop." She gave the woman a tiny shake. "Listen to me. It isn't Bertie. It's Charmaine."

Inside her skin, Jillian trembled like a dry leaf, but she maintained a firm grip, protecting her aunt. Cornelia gawped at the body—the pale face, the blue lips and dead eyes.

"Is she dead?" she choked out. "Check her, Jillian. Maybe she's just asleep."

Jillian had known on sight that Charmaine was dead, but she squatted and felt the pulse points on the cold neck. The artery was unmoving beneath her fingertips. The rain that had saturated the woman's garments had failed to completely wash away bloodstains on her silky pink pajama top.

"She's dead."

"What happened?" Cornelia gasped. "Did she fall? Did she have a heart attack?"

"I think someone must have . . ." Jillian stood, swallowing hard. She forced out the words. "Someone must have killed her."

"Killed her?" Cornelia swayed, legs giving way. Jillian caught her. "But how? Did someone shoot her?"

"Come on, let's go inside." Jillian struggled to get Cornelia away from the scene, but her aunt was determined to gawk at the body.

"Look," Cornelia said. "Look, she has something in her hand."

Before Jillian could stop her, Cornelia had snatched a scrap of paper from the dead woman's hand and thrust it into her pocket as if afraid of anyone seeing it.

"Aunt Cornelia! Give me that and don't touch anything else. I have to call the sheriff's office."

Jack and Bryce rushed out the door before Cornelia could respond.

"We thought we heard someone scream," Jack hollered as they ran toward the women.

"Help me get Aunt Cornelia into the house," she said as both men stumbled to a halt, eyes riveted on Charmaine's lifeless body. Bryce became stone immediately. She turned to Jack. "Take care of my aunt, please. I'll call the sheriff's office."

After one last devastated look, Jack nodded and put his arm around Cornelia's shoulders. With a firm but gentle effort, he turned her away and murmured quietly as he guided her back to the house. Inside, Dipsy Doodle howled as if she knew what they'd discovered. The dog must have witnessed whatever had happened to her owner. No wonder she'd been so terrified.

Jillian took the phone from her pocket and called the Nathan County Sheriff's Department. She struggled to keep her demeanor calm and controlled as she quickly relayed information to the dispatcher. The moment she pocketed her phone, Bryce broke out of his frozen state.

"I have to do something! Let me help her." He moved toward Charmaine.

Jillian made herself a barrier to the dead woman. "No, Bryce. The police are on their way."

"The law? No, no. Call an ambulance. Get that doctor who

makes house calls." He pointed a shaking finger at her. "Call someone *now*."

Jillian's ears rang, and she trembled so badly inside herself that she could hardly think, let alone speak. She forced out words. "I'm sorry, Bryce, but Charmaine's . . . gone."

He looked like a crazy man, eyes frantic, face burnished to a fiery hue. "What do you mean, 'gone'? She isn't gone. She's right there."

Why had no one ever prepared Jillian for a situation like this? Bryce looked near a breakdown. Should she call an ambulance for him? She tried to gulp in a deep breath but only gasped.

"Listen to me, Bryce." She grabbed his hands and squeezed them as hard as she could. "Look at me. Listen to what I'm telling you."

Somehow, in the depths of his panic and disbelief, he finally seemed to hear her. "Telling me?"

She kept hold of his hands and did her best to maintain eye contact with him. "I'm so sorry, Bryce. I wish I could—" He tried to move away. She shifted, staying between him and Charmaine's body. "Listen to me. There's no life left in her, Bryce. She's dead."

A long silence fell. "Dead?"

"Yes."

He remained in place, his gaze unwavering. Tremors ran through him worse than they shook her.

"Please tell me this is a bad dream," he whispered.

Her heart ached. "I wish I could. I am so, so sorry."

"She's really dead?"

"Yes."

Another long silence followed. He took a deep breath and pinned his gaze on Charmaine's body again. By slow degrees, she watched as the truth sank into his mind.

"What do you think happened?"

Before she could reply, Cornelia came out of the house and hurried toward them with Jack on her heels. She carried Dipsy Doodle cradled to her chest.

"I called Bertie, and she's on her way," she said. "Here, young man. This poor thing needs you." She handed the dog to Bryce.

Dipsy Doodle cuddled against him, burying her head under his arm as though hiding from the world. Bryce stared down at the furry bundle he held. He comforted her, his fingers gently smoothing and massaging.

Jillian had no idea what had transpired in the short time Cornelia and Jack had been gone, but apparently he had said something that soothed her. Or maybe talking to her twin sister on the phone was all the reassurance she'd needed.

Jillian's gaze fell on a wet splotch of the front of Cornelia's cherry-red apron pocket where the woman had stuffed the scrap of paper from Charmaine's hand. Anything that had been written on that paper might be a clue as to who killed Charmaine or why. Why on earth had Cornelia taken it? Did she know what was on that note? Didn't she realize the paper might hold important information that law enforcement would need? Or was it possible that she didn't want any authorities to know . . .?

Oh, for goodness' sake, stop it, Jillian. This is no time for wild imaginings, especially about your very own great-aunt.

Still, she couldn't dismiss the image of Cornelia snatching that scrap of paper.

Tires screeched in the driveway. A car door slammed loud enough to signal the Day of Doom. Thirty seconds later, Bertie came running into the back garden, her face full of alarm. Puffing and red-faced, she reached them.

"Oh my goodness, what's happened?"

The screaming wail of sirens grew louder as the police neared.

Breathing hard, Bertie stared at Charmaine. She leaned in and bent over, taking a closer look. She straightened, planting a palm against her heaving chest, and stood that way for a minute or so. Jillian watched with some concern until her grandmother's breathing slowed and the red began to ebb from her face.

Bertie pointed at the body and glared at Jillian. "How did this happen?"

Her grandmother's accusatory tone stunned Jillian. She wagged her mouth open and shut a couple of times.

"I don't . . . I didn't . . . Why are you looking at me like that? I'm pretty sure someone killed her, but it wasn't *me*, for goodness' sake."

Bertie blotted her forehead with a lace-trimmed hankie and then fanned her face with it.

"I never said it was *you*, Jillian, but you were here. You were the first one to get up this morning. Surely you saw something or someone."

She hated her grandmother's glower, but she held the woman's gaze. "I saw nothing unusual other than that poor little Dipsy Doodle outside on the veranda."

The sirens wailed to a stop at the side of the house.

"They're here," Jack said. "Shall I go get them?"

No one needed to escort the police. With long, purpose-filled steps, four of them—two men, two women—came around the house. To Jillian, they looked exactly like a striding line of actors on television cop shows. She almost expected to hear ominous theme music as they approached.

"Coy Henderson is back," Bertie said. "Thank goodness."

"Now we'll get something done," Cornelia said.

Every miscreant in Nathan County, Georgia, and probably some of the county officials wanted Sheriff Coy Henderson gone. He had passed retirement age more than five years ago, and that fact alone set some people's teeth on edge. He depended on a hearing aid, and his good health was uncertain.

Jillian had known Henderson since she was a child. Hard as nails, with a steel-trap mind, he excelled in his office. Deputies came and went, but Henderson remained, the rock that anchored county law enforcement year after year. Watching him now, noticing how his sharp eyes seemed to take in everything at once, Jillian could hardly believe the man had suffered a heart attack a few months earlier.

Surly-faced and stocky, the gray-haired sheriff marched toward them. His jaw was set, his gray-blue eyes colder than the steel barrel of the revolver strapped to his hip. He scowled at each person in turn as if taking mug shots with his eyes. His gaze then moved on to the body in the broken gardenia bushes. No one said a word as the quartet of law enforcement silently regarded the body as if viewing a sculpture in a museum.

A youngish, square-built woman with a block of short, black hair stood next to Henderson. She pulled on a pair of snug, blue latex gloves, wriggled her fingers a couple of times, and squatted beside Charmaine. She studied the bloodstain on the pink pajama top, then adjusted the garment to examine the damaged chest beneath it.

"Looks like she's been stabbed, Sheriff."

He stood over her, bending forty-five degrees from the waist, gazing at the wound. He nodded, and she stood.

"Get Hunter Greyson over here," he growled at her.

"But he'll only tell you what I—"

"Bogle, he's the county coroner, not you. Call him." He glared at the onlookers, his gaze stopping on Bertie. "Well, Bertie?"

She spread her hands, her face pale. "Sorry, Coy. I just got here myself. Jillian's the one who found her."

He turned to Jillian. When he scowled that way, his face had more wrinkles that Maudie Honeycutt's shar-pei.

"Tell me what you know," he said.

She hadn't seen Sheriff Henderson since she had moved back, and he still had the power to scare her.

"I found her body," she choked out, "just a few minutes ago. I'm the one who called your office."

Henderson squinted one eye at her as if trying to find a defect in the way her features were arranged. He stared at her so long, she squirmed.

"Stay right here, Jillian." He turned to the stocky female deputy. "Bogle," he barked, "I'm going to need statements from everyone, so get them away from the scene and into the house."

"Yes, sir." The woman seemed to blow up with self-importance. She held out both arms and flapped them toward the group like a crow trying to show off his size. "You heard the sheriff. Into the house. *All of you.*" She snapped her fingers at Jillian. "Inside."

"Bogle, can't you see I'm talking to this one?" He pinned his hard look at the woman as if wondering why he'd brought her along. To the other two deputies, "You two secure the scene." Once again, he turned to Jillian. "You say you found the body?"

She felt like she'd misbehaved by simply stepping outside that morning. "Yes, sir."

"Tell me." If nothing else, Coy Henderson would be remembered as a man of few words.

Choosing her own words with care and trying to leave nothing out, Jillian recounted everything, from hearing Dipsy Doodle yipping most of the night to discovering Charmaine's body.

She could nearly hear the clicking of his brain cells as he digested her words. As he stared at her, Jillian wondered if he was looking right through her.

"Anything else?" he said finally.

"No, sir."

Well, nothing else except Aunt Cornelia snatched a paper out of the dead woman's grip, and I know I should tell you about it, but then you might think she had something to do with this, and I can't let you interrogate her about it until I find out if that paper is important.

He asked no other questions, and he had taken no notes. "All right then."

He took her arm and led her as far as the veranda steps. Inside the living room, everyone stood at the large picture windows, watching the deputies work the scene. Deputy Bogle stood to one side where she could stand guard over the ones in the house while keeping an eye on the sheriff. She had one hand resting on the butt of her pistol as if she expected to hold off an entire gang of outlaws all alone.

"Go on inside now," he said to Jillian. His granite expression bore no yielding softness. "And I don't want any of y'all going anywhere for a bit."

"Yes, sir."

He looked past her and heaved a sigh that seemed to come up from the bottom of his boots.

"Bogle," he called as Jillian went inside. "Take your hand off your pistol and tell the folks in there not to leave Belle Haven."

She snapped to attention.

"All right, you people," she said, glaring at them, "orders from the sheriff: Nobody's to leave this room until further notice."

Bertie frowned and all but rolled her eyes. "What's going on out there?" she asked Jillian.

"That's official business." Bogle sniffed and shifted her posture until she stood, feet wide apart, hands on hips.

Bertie tightened her lips and turned back to Jillian. "What did Coy say to you?"

"He asked me when I found Charmaine and what I know."

"This is not for civilians to discuss," Bogle said, raising her voice and glowering. "You people get away from the window."

No one moved.

"As far as I know, we still have freedom of speech in this country," Bertie said. "We may talk about anything we want to. If you have a problem with that, go get Coy."

Bogle's right eye twitched.

"I'm not going to sit around in here like a ninny," Cornelia said. She headed toward the doorway.

"Hold it. Sheriff said you suspects are to go nowhere." Bogle's brown eyes glittered.

"*Suspects?*" Cornelia gaped at her.

"Sheriff Henderson meant we aren't to leave Belle Haven," Jillian said quickly.

"I don't care what he meant," Cornelia said shrilly. "Suspect, indeed." Her chin jutted at its most determined angle as she took a few steps to leave the room.

"I can't allow that," Bogle bellowed, moving toward her. "As long as I'm in charge, law and order will be observed."

"Now, you wait just a minute—"

The veranda door flew open, cutting off Jillian's words. Coy Henderson stood in the open doorway. So much for being hard of hearing. He must have had his hearing aid turned on high.

"Bogle. Outside. Now."

Some of the woman's bluster diminished as she turned and went outside.

"No one leaves this estate," Henderson said, running his gaze across each person in turn. "I'll be with you shortly."

"But, Coy," Bertie said, "I have to get back to the bakery. I have a business to run."

"Stay here." He slammed the door.

"Well, I declare." Bertie stared through the glass at his retreating back.

"That's no way to solve a crime." Cornelia glared outside and pointed. "That woman—'Tina Bogle' her tag said—has got a screw loose, mark my words. Telling us we were suspects, and she planned to have law and order. Strutting around like Barney Fife." She leaned forward to look out the window and then let out a little yelp. "Look at that! Ugly yellow tape all around my gardenias. Jillian, you go out there and tell them not to ruin my gardenias. Ask them if they have to have that tape in our garden. What a sight. What will the neighbors think?"

She rapped on the window. Henderson turned and glowered at her.

"Aunt Cornelia, they are our local law enforcement officers. I am not going to tell them how to do their job." She gave her great-aunt a sour look. "And I strongly encourage you not to order them about either." She forced a calm note into her voice. "Why don't you go upstairs and get your tatting basket? I'm sure you'll feel better about everything if you do some tatting. Remember you were going to trim the dish towels?"

Cornelia looked at her, blue eyes troubled. "Yes, that's a good idea. That's what I need to do." She left, muttering to herself. Jillian heard the names "Raymond" and "Possum" a couple of times before her great-aunt reached the landing and headed down the second floor hallway.

"Are you women forgetting Charmaine is dead?" Jack Porter burst out so suddenly he startled them. "Have you no heart or soul for her memory?"

"Of course we do," Jillian said gently. "I was trying to calm Aunt Cornelia."

"Poor Charmaine was our guest and our cousin," Bertie added. "We're extremely sorry for what's happened here. If we sounded heartless, please forgive us."

Her words, delivered quietly, brimmed with kindness, and he ducked his head.

"It's just . . ." He swallowed hard. "That's my Charmie out there, lying dead, and I don't understand why."

"None of us do right now, Jack."

"I know. I'm . . ." He put one hand to his forehead. "I'm sorry."

"Don't worry about it," Jillian said. "You're upset. We all are."

Bryce turned from the window. Rubbing Dipsy Doodle's head, he stared around the room as if he'd forgotten where he was. He moved woodenly toward an armchair, sitting down and holding the dog close.

"Look," Bertie said suddenly. "Tom Shaw has found something." The deputy was putting a pair of gardening scissors in an evidence bag.

Are those the missing scissors Aunt Cornelia had mentioned? Jillian thought. Hadn't she said she had used them recently but couldn't remember what she'd done with them? Where had the deputy found them, and why was he putting them in a bag? Staring at the bag that held the scissors gave her a sick feeling that started in her stomach and worked its way into every cell of her body.

"They'll bag up every little scrap and tidbit they find." She sounded a lot steadier than she felt.

"I don't see how they can find much, what with all the rain washing everything to kingdom come," Bertie said, still frowning and watching the activity outside. "Do they know what happened to Charmaine?" Before Jillian could respond, her grandmother continued, as if talking to herself. "It wasn't an accident, was it? Not with crime-scene tape blocking the area. And scissors in an evidence bag. No, that wouldn't be an accident."

Jillian shuddered, remembering the torn pajama top with stains the rain hadn't washed away.

A familiar figure joined the team outside. Tall and muscular, educated and professional, Hunter Greyson was well-suited to the position of the Nathan County coroner. Jillian hoped she could get some of the desired information out of him. Right then, though, she knew it was best to let the law do its job. With Henderson barking orders, Deputy Laura Lee Zane took photos of the area around Charmaine, then photographed her from every angle. Deputy Shaw pointed at the ground in different areas, talking with Hunter. Tina Bogle prowled the garden and poked into the gardenias.

"Look at that mess," Cornelia screeched as she came back into the room with her tatting basket. "See? I knew it. They are going to ruin my gardenias. Lookee there. That woman policeman is shoving herself right into that bush."

Jillian caught Cornelia's hand just before her aunt tapped on the window glass. "Finding out what happened to Charmaine and who killed her is more important than your gardenias. I know you're upset. We all are. But getting in a tizzy, yelling at the sheriff, and making demands are going to hurt us far more than help us. In fact, let's step away from the window and have some coffee. Come on, everyone." She turned and held out an arm, beckoning them from the window.

Bryce never moved in his chair.

"Bryce?" Jillian said in some alarm. "Are you all right?"

He said nothing.

Of course he's not all right. Whether Charmaine was sweet and kindly or gruff and bossy was immaterial at that moment. The two had been close, and he had been devoted to her.

Or so it had seemed.

But maybe not . . .

The front door opened, and a familiar voice called out.

"Hello! It's me. What's going on?" Heels clicked rapidly on the polished wooden floor of the foyer, then Savannah rushed into the living room. "I heard sirens in town but had no idea they were coming to Belle Haven until I got here." She ran a panicked look at Cornelia and Bertie as if to assure herself they were well and safe. "What's going on?"

"It's that woman. Our cousin." Cornelia pointed out the window.

"What about her? Is she hurt?"

"She's dead." The words dropped from Bertie's lips like two stones.

Savannah's eyes rounded. "What? When? How?"

"We aren't sure," Jillian said. She glanced at Bryce's frozen face, then Jack's ghostly white one. This was not the place to speculate aloud. "I was about to make some coffee. Come help me, Savannah."

In the kitchen, Savannah said, "What in the world, Jillian?" She kept her bewildered voice quiet.

"I don't know much. Right now, it's all so surreal."

"Tell me what you *do* know."

Jillian glanced toward the door into the living room and pulled Savannah farther into the kitchen. In an undertone, while she made coffee, she told Savannah the events of that morning.

"Deputy Bogle looked at the body and said she'd been stabbed, but I don't know. She seems overeager, as if she hopes to see crime where none exists, but . . ."

"But?"

"I saw the body. Up close. Charmaine's pajama top was torn, and there was blood. At least some blood stains."

"Is it possible Charmaine slipped in the mud and fell against something and tore her clothes? Or maybe she had an aneurism, and it caused her to fall. Maybe she had something to drink, or took some pills, or something."

Jillian admitted her friend had a valid point, but something told her Savannah's guesses were wrong.

"Hunter will make that determination, I assume, and he's out there right now." She looked out the back windows near the breakfast table. "I told you there was something off about that woman."

"Something to get her killed?"

"Yes."

"But who? I mean . . . other than you, Bertie, and Cornelia, there was no one else here last night except Charmaine and Bryce. Right?"

"Right." Jillian could practically see the gears in Savannah's brain churning and steaming.

"I can't imagine Bryce . . . that is, goodness gracious, Jillian. Do you think he could, um, you know . . . ?" She made a slashing gesture across her throat. "He seems like such a mild-mannered guy."

"I agree. Bryce is almost a Caspar Milquetoast, but Charmaine was so mean to him. Didn't you notice?"

"Oh, I noticed all right."

"Maybe he finally had enough."

The two women looked at each other, thinking about that.

"You have a point," Savannah said.

"Yes, I do." Jillian took several mugs from the cabinet and placed them on two serving trays. For a moment, she gazed at the tray she'd used for Charmaine the day before. A shiver slid down her backbone. "But I'm pretty sure he didn't leave Dipsy Doodle outside in the rain and leave her alone all night. He and that dog love each other."

"Well, then." Savannah made a loose gesture as if brushing dust away from her. "There you go. Do you think a devoted dog lover could kill someone?"

"I'm sure a lot of murderers are dog lovers. A lot of people like dogs better than humans. Don't you ever watch true-crime shows on television?"

"Not if I can help it." Savannah paused. "But then, when you think about it, Jillian, who else could have killed her? I mean, if someone actually did."

Jillian turned from fixing the coffee and faced her.

"That's what I'm saying. What if . . ." She lowered her voice to a mere whisper. "What if we have a murderer sitting in our front room right this very minute?"

"But there is only Bertie, Cornelia, Bryce, and Jack."

"Exactly."

The two women stared at each other wide-eyed.

"Good gravy," Savannah replied in a whisper.

"Exactly," Jillian whispered back. "What am I supposed to do? How do I protect my grandmother and my great-aunt?"

Savannah held up one hand, her expression thoughtful. "Wait. Before you say anything to anyone, let's think this out a minute. Remember you told me you thought Charmaine probably held something over Bryce. That 'something' is probably why he has stayed with her in spite of her meanness."

Jillian nodded. "We need to find out what that 'something' was."

"Yes. And I think you're the one to do it."

"And I think you need to help me." Jillian filled all the cups on the tray. "Hand me the cookie jar, will you?"

"It's too early to serve cookies."

Jillian gave her an exasperated look and arranged the treats on two separate plates.

"I know Coy Henderson. He is not going to come skipping in here and tell us anything. But maybe someone will share something, especially if I offer them some of Bertie's Gone to Heaven cookies."

Savannah winced. "I realize those cookies belong in paradise, but I don't think you should refer to them as 'Gone to Heaven' cookies when you offer them—not with a dead body lying right there. In fact, it seems a little tacky to be serving refreshments over a corpse."

Jillian loved Savannah dearly, but sometimes her friend had a remarkable lack of imagination. She added napkins and a plate of cookies on each tray.

"Let's see what we can figure out or overhear while we pass around the coffee and cookies, then let's caucus to form a plan of action."

"You sound like a politician."

"That's unfortunate." She picked up one of the trays, and Savannah got the other one. "What I want you to do is pay attention to both Bryce and Jack. Jack seemed to have recovered from shock in record speed. Besides, he could have easily come back in the middle of the night."

"And what? Lured her outside?" Savannah shook her head. "She made it clear the minute he showed up that she was going to have nothing to do with him, so I hardly think she would have answered his phone call, let alone gone outside to meet him. In the pouring rain. In the middle of the night."

Jillian twisted her mouth, knowing her friend had a valid point. "Just watch him, okay? Talk to him. Talk to Bryce."

"And then we caucus?"

"And then we caucus."

With the full, heavy tray balanced in her grip, Jillian made her way down the veranda steps toward the crime scene.

"Hold it!" Henderson yelled, glaring at her. He ducked beneath the crime-scene tape and strode toward her. "What do you think you're doing?"

She froze in place, feeling like she'd been caught picking his pocket or something even more nefarious. Hunter looked up from the body only long enough to give her a short nod of greeting.

"I thought your team might like some coffee. And some cookies."

"We're here to work, not party," Bogle said, coming to stand beside Henderson as if he needed her support.

Henderson glanced at her, then spoke over his shoulder. "Zane, show Bogle how to use the camera."

"But I already know how to—"

The sheriff's stony expression clearly said he'd listen to no argument. Not from Bogle, not from Jillian. Not from anyone, ever.

"We're in the middle of an investigation," he growled, but it was a quiet growl, as if he was trying to understand why she brought refreshments to a crime scene.

Jillian took heart. Besides, she wasn't going to back down without at least trying to learn something new.

"Coffee usually has a bracing, energizing effect. Sugar too. I thought you and the deputies might need that."

The soft spring breeze stirred the aroma of the coffee, and all three deputies glanced longingly toward Jillian's offering. Henderson scowled at the tray, then nodded once.

"All right. Coffee. No cookies." She took a step, but he stopped her. "Stand there." He beckoned the deputies. "One cup. Drink it here, no lingering."

Jillian smiled at each one. Even Tina Bogle, whose grimace could have been a smile or a dirty look.

"Thank you, Jillian." Laura Lee Zane gave her a quick smile. Young and energetic, Laura Lee was a member of the Sweetie Pies as well as a Nathan County deputy.

"How's it going?" Jillian asked.

"All right," replied Shaw. "The mud makes it difficult."

"Yes. You people and your footprints are all over the place." Bogle slurped her coffee, eyeing the crime scene as if she expected Jillian to go stomping around it. "The murder weapon was covered with muck and mud."

Jillian nearly dropped the tray. "Murder weapon?"

"Bogle!" Henderson grabbed the nearly empty cup from her hands and banged it down on the tray.

"I . . . I . . ." The woman looked as if she was about to cry, and Jillian nearly felt sorry for her.

The sheriff rubbed his temples with one hand. "Bogle, go practice taking photos."

"Yes, sir," she said meekly and joined Laura Lee.

Jillian thought about the scissors she'd seen go in the evidence bag. Whether the sheriff would answer her or not remained to be seen, but she had to ask. "You found a murder weapon?"

Henderson continued to rub one side of his head, then finally dropped his hand. He let out a long breath and spoke quietly.

"Listen, Bogle is new. A rookie. She's long on ambition and short on sense, and she's watched way too many cop shows for too long. It's best to ignore her."

"I understand."

He nodded. "Good."

Jillian's mind went back to the garden scissors, and on the heels of that, she thought of the sodden scrap of paper Cornelia had snatched from Charmaine's lifeless hand. She thought of her great-aunt's animosity toward Charmaine and how she wanted the woman gone. Jillian wanted to talk, to clear the air, to reassure herself Cornelia had nothing to do with Charmaine's death, but the words stuck in her throat. She felt sick.

Hunter walked toward them, pulling off his blue gloves. Behind him, the transport vehicle with Charmaine's body inside drove away. He signed a paper and handed it to the sheriff, whose attention had been captured by his deputies. Henderson's scowl deepened, and he stalked toward them.

"Good morning, Jillian," Hunter said, smiling slightly. "That coffee looks great and smells even better."

"Help yourself."

"I've got to get back to my office, but I'll go say hello to your great-aunt and grandmother, if that's all right." He took the tray from her.

Jillian wasn't sure if he was being kind or if he was politely taking her away from law enforcement. She glanced behind and saw Henderson chewing out Tina Bogle again. Jillian wondered if the woman would be able to stand up under such a hard job and demanding taskmaster.

Jillian and Hunter reached the veranda door, and Bertie opened it. She, Cornelia, and Jack surrounded them, spewing questions at Hunter like a bottle of warm, shaken soda pop. With considerable patience and gentle regard for everyone's state of mind, he evaded their questions and assured them the authorities had everything under control.

"Sheriff Henderson or one of his deputies will talk to you when the time is right. It's early in the investigation yet."

"I hope he doesn't send that goofy woman in here to talk to us," Cornelia fretted as she sat down and picked up a half-edged pillowcase. "Why, she'd as soon throw us all in the lockup as not."

"Now, Aunt Cornelia," Jillian said, "she's new on the job."

"*Humph*." Cornelia bent her head over her work and said nothing more.

Jillian gazed at the hoary head and that tense, energetic body and felt a rush of love. She had to get to the bottom of this whole ugly mess and, if need be, protect her great-aunt from the fallout.

She walked with Hunter to the front door.

"Can you tell me how Charmaine died?" she asked him in an undertone.

He raised one eyebrow.

"I saw her pajama top had been torn and some blood . . ." she whispered.

"What did you think might have happened to her?"

"I'm not sure, but I think . . ." She leaned closer. "I think someone might have, well, probably *killed* her. You know. Stabbed her. Or something."

He hesitated, then said, "I'd say you're on the right track."

Although Jillian had been sure of this, his agreement brought a cold shiver down her spine.

"Do you know what she was stabbed with? I mean, a knife probably. Right?"

"I'm sending her body on to the crime lab, but from what I saw, I'd say something heavy, something never meant to be used as a shiv."

"Tina Bogle said the murder weapon had been found."

He gave her a smile and leaned toward her. "Between you and me, Tina Bogle has a lot to learn," he said near her ear.

"That's what Sheriff Henderson said."

"He wouldn't say it if he didn't mean it."

"I know."

"We're still on for Saturday, right?" he asked before he stepped outside.

"Absolutely. I'm looking forward to it."

He touched her upper arm, just for a moment, in a gesture of friendship and support. "Hang in there, Jillian. Coy Henderson will get to the bottom of this in short order. See you later."

She watched him go and prayed he was right.

"Time to caucus?"

Savannah's stage whisper right behind her startled Jillian enough that she jumped. She told herself she had to calm down. Too much depended on her having a level head.

"Don't you need to get back to work?"

"Let me worry about that."

"But—"

"I'm overdue for some time off, so hush. I'm here to help. Let me."

"If we hang out down here, we're going to be interrupted every two minutes. Let's go upstairs to my room and hope no one sees us making our exit."

Their stealthy retreat from the living room came to a halt halfway up the steps when the sheriff strode inside with something in his hand. He scoured the room with his eyes, his gaze landing on Jillian.

"You. Jillian. Let's talk."

It seemed the library was the quietest and most logical place to be interrogated unless, as Henderson put it, anyone wanted to "go with me downtown." Everyone knew he didn't mean go downtown for a bite of lunch or a little bit of shopping.

He settled behind the desk, ignoring the dust.

"Would you like a cup of coffee? Or a glass of sweet tea?" Jillian asked. After all, she'd been raised to offer anyone in her home at least a beverage before conversation.

"No. Sit." He pointed to a nearby wing chair and gestured for her to pull it closer to the desk. He laid the bagged garden scissors on top of the desk and put his hat on top of the bag, disguising the contents. "Tell me again this morning's events, in order."

Jillian gave the hat one goggle-eyed glance, as though the scissors beneath it squatted there, like a spider ready to pounce. She carefully kept her gaze off of them. She settled nervously into the chair. Taking her time, she recounted what had happened.

Henderson listened, his gaze fixed on her face. He didn't blink, and as before, he didn't take notes. "Did you know this woman before she showed up on Sunday?"

"I'd never seen her before, nor even heard of her. And neither had my grandmother or my great-aunt. Charmaine said she was a relative from Virginia, but I'm not so sure." Henderson raised one eyebrow, and she continued. "She seemed phony most of the time, going overboard with Southernisms and an accent that was inconsistent. She told us a story about one of our ancestors, Captain Hoyt Belle. He's the one who built this house."

She paused, wondering if she needed to clarify further. Henderson gestured for her to keep talking.

"She told us she was the descendant of his third wife, who was much younger than the captain and the daughter of a local pig farmer. The thing is, as I said before, none of us—that is, Bertie, Aunt Cornelia, nor I—had ever heard of this third wife, Flora. And the more we asked about her, the more outrageous Charmaine's story became."

Once again Jillian paused, wondering if she was babbling. She asked herself how much information the sheriff needed, but he simply stared at her, obviously expecting a full report.

"I looked at the local history book in the library, and I searched online. I found nothing to substantiate her claim."

His expression changed, his frown deepening. "Why is this relevant?"

"I'm not sure it *is* relevant to her murder. But I do wonder why she pretended to be related to us if she wasn't."

For the first time, Henderson pulled a small notebook from his pocket and jotted something down.

"Did you hear or see anything in the middle of last night that roused your concern?"

"Not really."

"No one creeping around in the house, no one outside?"

"There was the storm, after all. Raining beating against the house, lightning and thunder."

"But the storm stopped about three o'clock."

"Did it?"

He stared at her, like a bird of prey, waiting for her to stumble and fall so he could swoop in and pick at her remains.

"There was one time when I heard a door open and close upstairs, and someone in the corridor." His face never softened, not even a little. She wished he'd at least blink. "My bedroom is up there, and that's why I heard it. That must've been after the storm."

"And . . .?"

"And?"

"And what did you do? Did you get up to see who was in the corridor at some time after two or three in the morning?"

"No. I figured it was Bryce or Charmaine taking the dog out. Dipsy Doodle—that's the dog's name—was barking some during the storm."

"And that's when you got up to check on her?"

She'd already told the man all this, and it occurred to her that someone as sharp as Coy Henderson was also cagey. He was testing her story to see if it remained consistent or if she made up new details.

"No, sir. I got up, showered, dressed, went downstairs, and realized Dipsy Doodle was outside. And had been outside for quite a while." She tipped her head to one side, meeting his eyes straight on. "Sheriff Henderson, it seems unlikely that someone as spoiled as Charmaine Rawlins would get up in the middle of the night and take her dog out. She would have awakened Bryce to do it for her. There had to be a reason, something far more personal to her, than a dog who needed to relieve itself."

One corner his mouth twitched. "And what reason would that have been?"

She spread her hands and shook her head. "I don't know. I'm telling you, the woman was a virtual stranger to us."

"And yet you took her into your home."

"Well, you know Bertie and Cornelia."

The gimlet-eyed stare again, probing to see if she was being truthful?

"I'm pretty sure, though, all three of us had our suspicions."

"You had suspicions that she wasn't who she said she was." He said it flat out, not as a question.

"Right."

She squirmed as he continued to gaze at her, pilfering her brain, cataloging its contents, separating gold from trash.

She uncrossed and recrossed her ankles.

He tapped one finger on the arm of the chair.

She cleared her throat and straightened her spine.

He sighed. A long, deep, lingering exhalation that Jillian thought would surely deplete his body of all oxygen.

"Out with it," he said.

Her heart faltered. "Huh?"

"You'd be better off telling me everything now, Jillian. I'm going to get to it, sooner or later."

She gulped. Of course he would. But how did he know she was hiding something?

15

"I wouldn't say that I'm hiding anything," she said.

He never blinked.

"I've told you everything I know about Charmaine. If anyone—"

There was rap on one of the library doors, then it opened, and Cornelia entered, pushing the tea cart in front of her.

"Excuse me," she said as she wheeled the squeaky cart right up to the desk. "We're getting so many callers that we decided to make more refreshments for everyone. Sheriff, would you prefer tea or coffee? We have all kinds of cake and cookies, and Bertie is making sandwiches— "

"Cornelia, I'm in the middle of questioning your niece."

"Thank you, Aunt Cornelia," Jillian said, jumping up. She clasped the woman's upper arm gently and tried to steer her toward the door. "Now, why don't you go help Bertie?" In an undertone, she added, "Don't come in here again."

"But it's my duty as hostess to serve refreshments to our guests, and oh, they are piling up."

"Why? Who's out there?" Henderson stood.

"That boy who writes items for the *Moss Hollow Chronicle*. And a reporter from one of the newspapers somewhere near Savannah. Oh, and a couple of women from the Sweetie Pies. I'm sure more will come. You know how folks around here are. Every little tragedy and triumph is a reason to bring food."

The "boy" who wrote items for the *Chronicle* was in late middle age, but Jillian chose not to point out the fact.

"Oh, for the love of Mike." Coy pushed back his chair and

strode out of the library, leaving the doors wide open. "Rod Douglas, you newspaper people could double as cadaver dogs, the way you sniff out dead bodies."

"Sheriff," Douglas said, "what can you tell us about this death? Is it true the victim was found murdered in the flower garden out back? How was she killed? When?"

Henderson grumbled and growled a response, which sounded to Jillian as if he planned to be as evasive as possible for as long as possible. While he was busy with the reporter, she closed the library door and pulled Cornelia to one side.

"Listen," she said in a near whisper, although the library was virtually soundproof, "you've had a rough morning. Why don't you slip up the back stairs to your room and take a nap?"

"*Take a nap?*" As if she'd never heard of such a thing. Cornelia shook off Jillian's clasp and returned to the tea cart. "Shall I pour you tea or coffee? And Maudie brought some of her spice cake. You know how much you love it."

She held up a small plate with a generous golden-brown slice on it. Even if Jillian had been on the other side of the room, she could have smelled the cinnamon and cloves. She did have a weakness for spice cakes, and the spicier, the better.

"Okay, then. Leave the cake. But if you don't want to take a nap, maybe you can go to your room and tat. You always say it relaxes you."

Cornelia put a fist on each hip and frowned at her. "What in the world is wrong with you? Yes, it's been an upsetting morning, but we have guests out there, and I'm not going to go sneaking off to my room to nap, or to tat."

For the first time, she noticed Cornelia was wearing a frilly apron with bluebirds and roses on it.

"Where is that red apron you were wearing when we were outside?"

"Why, it was dirty, so I took it off. It's in the laundry hamper in the mudroom. Why?"

Jillian shot a look at the library door, leaned close, and whispered, "What did you do with that paper?"

"What paper?" Cornelia said in her everyday, out-loud voice.

Jillian flinched. "Shh. Not so loud. That paper you took from Charmaine's hand."

A strange expression fell over the woman's face. "Oh, that. I did nothing with it. Why?"

"We need to get it before Sheriff Henderson comes back in here."

Cornelia blinked at her. "You think it might be important?"

"Of course it's important. Think about it. Why did Charmaine have it clutched in her hand when she died? There's got to be something written on it that—"

The door opened, and Henderson came back into the room. He stared hard at both women as he returned to the desk chair.

"Cake and coffee, Coy?" Cornelia asked brightly.

"What are you two talking about?" His sharp eyes shifted back and forth between both faces. Then he leaned back in the chair, interlocked his fingers as if he had all the time in the world to sit there, and added, "Jillian, I believe I know why you're hiding something, and she's standing right in front of me with a piece of cake."

Cornelia's mouth flew open, and she set down the plate with a clunk.

"Hiding something?" Cornelia said. "Who? Me? I'm not hiding a blessed thing. I forgot about it, that's all."

"Forgot what?"

"That piece of paper I took, of course."

He narrowed his eyes. "What piece of paper?"

"The one in Charmaine's hand."

If Henderson's frown got any deeper, it would cut right smack into his skull.

"Shall I go fetch it, Coy?"

"Yes. Do that." He fixed his glare on Jillian. "You. Stay right here."

"But I—"

"Stay." He did not drop his gaze or blink. "Sit." He pointed at the wing chair without looking at it. "There."

Jillian obeyed, but not without some rebellion stirring. She told herself he was not trying to sound as if he were giving orders to a Labrador retriever. This was his way of communicating.

Still. He could at least add a "please" or "thank you" here or there.

"I knew you were hiding something."

If only knowing about that paper was all I was hiding.

Without conscious volition, her gaze strayed to his hat. "She's my great-aunt, and she's elderly. I love her. What was I supposed to do? Bring you her head on a platter?"

"Of course not. I understand how you feel."

He did? "You do?"

"But this is a homicide investigation. I can't turn a blind eye to evidence or ignore it when someone is trying to keep something from me."

Jillian crimped her lips tight, determined to say nothing else.

Henderson surprised her by reaching for a serving of cake and taking a bite. "Not bad. Maudie knows how to make a spice cake."

Why hadn't he mentioned the scissors? They were right there. Maybe he was waiting for her, or daring her, to mention them first.

Jillian refused to indulge him and get herself caught up in his wily game. She pinned her gaze on the cold fireplace and tried not to think of what had happened in the last few hours. It flooded her mind anyway: Charmaine's death; Cornelia's open antipathy toward Charmaine, Bryce, and Dipsy Doodle; and her wish that they would all go away, and *soon*. Killing Charmaine certainly got her out of the way, soon. The paper Cornelia grabbed. All of it created a box of suspicion around the elderly woman.

Jillian did her best to shove those unsettling notions from her mind so they didn't show on her face like a big inky smear only the sheriff could see. She shifted in the chair and ducked her head, but she could feel his probing, all-seeing gaze on her.

"Here it is," Cornelia said, hurrying through the door. She waved the scrap of paper in the air. "It's dry now, but not going to do you a lick of good."

Henderson frowned and took it from her.

"What does it say, Aunt Cornelia?" Jillian asked.

"Nary a thing. Not a blessed word. That girl was holding a blank note."

Henderson squinted at the paper. He got up and walked to the window, where he examined it every way possible in the sunlight.

"If there was ever anything on it," Cornelia said, "the rain washed it away."

"The rain left traces of blood on Charmaine's shirt," Jillian said. "I saw that myself. Surely there is something on that paper that will help you, Sheriff."

It seemed Henderson almost smiled, but probably not. He was probably grimacing in pain. He pulled a plastic bag from his pocket and placed the note in it, then he dragged a wing chair from its place near a bookshelf and settled it close to the one where Jillian sat. Once more, he sat behind the desk and eyed them both. The room no longer felt like an old library. It felt like an interrogation room.

"This is Moss Hollow," he said. "We aren't exactly CSI around here. Have a seat, Cornelia, and tell me why you took this paper from her hand."

Cornelia's mouth flew open, but no words came out. Henderson did not move, not a twitch, not a blink. She tried to speak again and failed.

"You had no way of knowing this was blank. You obviously were looking for something."

Cornelia sputtered again and scowled at him. "Oh, for pity's sake. I don't know why I took it. I suppose I thought she might have written something important. Sometimes I get these feelings. You know that."

Uh-oh. Please don't start talking about Possum's psychic abilities and Uncle Raymond's wisdom.

Apparently he had heard about Cornelia's otherworldly leanings, because all he uttered was a skeptical, "Mmm-hmm."

She huffed. "Well, what do you want me to say? That I thought the note held the formula to a magical youth serum? Or maybe that it was a note about me and where I hid the family fortune?"

"Did it?"

She sputtered some more, and her creased face reddened. This alarmed Jillian. She leaned forward and gripped her great-aunt's cold hand.

"Sheriff, I think you need to let Aunt Cornelia—"

Cornelia snatched her hand free. "Jillian, will you stop looking at me like that? I'm fine." She turned her dark glare to the poker-faced lawman. "Forevermore, Coy Henderson. If you have such fool notions running through your skull, then you really do need to hang up your sheriff's badge the way some folks around here say. I'm telling you, I saw that paper, and I grabbed it. I don't know why. I just did it."

His expression remained stolid. Well, except for a slight flicker in his eyes.

"Were you up and around last night?" he asked her.

"You mean in the middle of the night?"

He nodded once.

"Not at all. That storm and those awful people in our house . . ." She threw up both hands in a helpless gesture. "Bertie and I were so upset, we both took one of those sleeping pills Maddie Workhouse sells over there at her health-food store. I was out like a light in no time, and I don't believe I stirred the whole night." She scooted forward in her seat. "I'll tell you who you need to look at, Coy." She rapped her knuckles on the desktop three times. "That Bryce person whom she treated like a dog."

"Oh, now, Aunt Cornelia, I hardly think Sheriff Henderson—"

"He might look as meek and mild as a lamb," Cornelia said, "but I've looked into his eyes. I've seen. Some people can be read like a book, if you know when to look and how to listen." She shook her index finger at Henderson. "You know exactly what I mean, Coy. That's why you're so good at this job."

Henderson turned his calculating look on Jillian. If he thought she was going to cast any further suspicions on her great-aunt, he was sadly mistaken. After all, she hadn't gotten up to see who was in the corridor in the wee hours, and it might have been Cornelia. She remained as impassive as possible and dared not even glance at the concealing hat on the desk.

"You may go," he said to Jillian.

"I'll stay here with Aunt Cornelia." She reached over and patted Cornelia's hand.

"No, you won't. Go."

"But . . ."

He lifted one brow, and she figured he was half a breath away from escorting her out of the room if she didn't leave right then.

"Oh, go on," Cornelia said. "I'm not afraid of him. I remember when he got caught spray-painting 'Coy loves Janie' on the water tower."

Jillian couldn't stop the grin that spread across her face. "Really?"

Henderson's face turned red beneath his scowl. "I was seventeen," he snapped.

"Yes, with hair clear past your shoulders and the most pitiful attempt at a beard."

"Oh, my," Jillian said. She bit her lip to keep from giggling.

"You. Out. Now."

"Go, Jillian, before you cause more trouble. And take the tea cart with you."

Before I *cause more trouble?*

16

Jillian pulled the library door shut behind her and halted with one hand on the tea cart, the other resting on the heavy doorknob. The room around her was filled with sound, and those sounds came from the living room. The library was so quiet that if Jillian hadn't known better, she would have thought Belle Haven was nearly deserted. A look around the room showed her several members of the Sweetie Pies stood or sat, chatting, snacks in hand.

Rod Douglas and a middle-aged woman Jillian didn't recognize mingled with the others. Each held a camera in one hand and a notebook in the other. A third person, a woman, a much younger reporter—because it was obvious that was who comprised this little group—held a small notebook and a cell phone. The fourth member of the journalistic persuasion, gray-haired and rather short and stout, stood slightly apart, his expression aloof as he jotted down notes.

Savannah moved among the guests, a coffeepot in one hand and a pitcher of icy sweet tea in the other.

"There's Bertie's granddaughter, Jillian Green," Wanda Jean Maplewood said rather loudly to the gray-haired overweight reporter. She pointed. "She lives here. And *she's* the one who found the body."

The man turned, but the other three reached her first. They crowded around her as close as possible with the tea cart in the way.

"Is it true you found the deceased?" the youngest one asked.

"How do you feel, being the one who found—?" the other woman began.

"How was she killed? Did you know her? Why was she here in Belle Haven?" the older man interrupted without looking up. He was busy scribbling something.

Rod Douglas, sporting faded bushy red hair and woolly eyebrows, spoke up. "Did you have anything to do with her death?"

The gray-haired heavy-set man of the group started to speak but dropped his notes, then clambered awkwardly to hang on to his pen and camera as he retrieved the notebook.

Jillian stared at all four of them. With the exception of the older man who continued to fumble, all of them had their pencils, cameras, and, in one case, phone pointed and poised, ready to record her words.

"Sheriff Henderson has already spoken to you, and I'm not saying anything at this time."

"Why's that?" Douglas asked. "Do you have information law enforcement refuses to disclose?"

"Our readers deserve to know the truth!" the young woman piped up.

She tried to move away from them and even nudged the old guy with the tea cart, but they were disinclined to step back. Instead, they threw another barrage of questions at her. Their faces, voices, smells, and nervous energy mingled around her, mixing with the stares and anticipation from the Sweetie Pies and the odor of baked goods. Jillian's stomach lurched.

"Just go, please. There really is nothing any of us can say right now. If you want to leave your cards on the table in the foyer, maybe one of us will call you when we are allowed to do so. But only if you go right now."

Pencils scratched against paper, cameras clicked, flashes flashed, but no one moved toward the door.

"Listen," Jillian said in her loudest, sternest, rather angry tone, "I didn't want to say this, but I've asked you to go, and you haven't. You are now trespassing, and I'm within my rights to call the sheriff's department, again." She caught Savannah's eye. "Will you call 911, please?"

"Absolutely." She set down the beverage containers on the cart and took her cell phone from the pocket of her slacks. "Calling right now." She paused, finger above the screen. "Or we could ask the sheriff to get the deputies back on the scene. They left only a couple of minutes ago and could be here in a flash."

That seemed to do the trick. She and Savannah stood, side by side, at the open front door until the final one had stepped outside. Jillian closed and locked the door.

"Cornelia is still in the library with the sheriff," she said. "He refused to let me stay with her."

"He's a hard man," Savannah said. "That's why he's such a good sheriff."

"But—"

"She'll be okay, but if you'd like, I can pop my head in and check on her."

Savannah knew nothing about the garden scissors. Jillian saw no reason to layer more suspicion on her great-aunt.

"That would be good. Thank you." She glanced around the room. "Where's Bertie?"

"Where do you think? In the kitchen, of course. In fact, she chased that old reporter out with a rolling pin in her hand. Not raised, of course. I think she was making a piecrust."

"I have a perfect view of the dining room sideboard from here. With all the food I see, why is she baking more, bless her heart? Excuse me, Savannah."

She dashed into the kitchen. The laughter coming from the room confused her only slightly less than seeing Bertie and a petite blonde at the stove, looking down at whatever had just been pulled from the oven. The heat and humidity of the room nearly pushed Jillian back out the door.

"My very first pie," the blonde sang out, sending her and Bertie into more giggles.

The smell of chocolate, tomatoes, onions, peppermint, and fish greeted Jillian like a bad dream she'd had one too many times. Jillian blinked hard, trying to clear her vision, but the steamy, messy kitchen did not change, nor did the presence of a disheveled strange woman at the stove with her grandmother.

"Bertie?" She passed a stunned gaze around the room. "The sideboard in the dining room is full of cakes and pies. Every flat surface in the kitchen is covered with food."

"Yes, dear."

"Excuse me, but I have a couple of questions. The first one is why are you cooking so much? The second is"—she turned to the blonde—"who are you?"

"For goodness' sake, Jillian," Bertie said, her smile slipping. "There is a nicer way of meeting someone than that. This is Kandi Kerber. She has been my right arm for the last few hours."

"Bertie was up to her eyebrows when I got here, so I put my work aside to help her." She favored the older woman with an affectionate smile. "She reminds me so much of my own grandmother. Any time Granny got under stress, she either cleaned until the house shone like new glass, or she cooked until there was nothing left in the house to fry, bake, or boil."

The two women laughed as if sharing a fabulous joke. Jillian blinked hard at them.

"I haven't cooked *all* this in the last two hours, if that's what you're thinking," Bertie said. "The Sweetie Pies made most of it. Kandi and I put together some things for lunch, though. We have a lot of people to feed. But when Kandi said she'd never made an apple pie in her life, I told her it was high time she learned while she was here."

"But Bertie!" Jillian winced at the shrill whine that issued from her mouth. She cleared her throat. "There's a murder investigation going on. I kicked out a whole slew of nosy reporters."

"You did?" Bertie and Kandi said at the same time.

"I did. Honestly, Bertie, do you think Charmaine's death is a reason to have a party? Or to give cooking lessons?"

How Bertie was able to look surprised and offended at the same time was a secret only she knew.

"In the first place, Jillian Green, this is *not* a party, and you know it. You know full well how the Sweetie Pies try to help with food in time of crisis. Any crisis." She gave Jillian what some folks might call the stink eye. "In the second place, Kandi has been a godsend." Bertie pointed to the sink. "This girl has washed every dish, fork, cup, and glass that has come through that door. Dried them and got them ready to use again, in a quarter of the time it would have taken to run the dishwasher."

"Maybe she would be of help in the bakery then. Poor Lenora and Maggie are probably exhausted if the reporters and other curiosity seekers have invaded The Chocolate Shoppe the way they have Belle Haven."

"I closed the bakery." Bertie's voice was cool and matter-of-fact.

Jillian gaped her. "You did? When?"

"When it was apparent Coy Henderson and his band of merry men and women were going to be here for goodness knows how long. And then Lenora called and said people were coming in, talking and asking a lot of questions, some of them following her back into the kitchen and snooping around."

"Reporters?"

"Lots of folks. Busybodies. I saw no reason for poor Lenora to be hassled into exhaustion."

"But aren't we going to lose business?"

"We can afford to be closed the odd day." Bertie's expression said the subject of the bakery had come to an end. "And I'll thank you to be a little more gracious in the future." She turned to Kandi, who had silently taken in the exchange. "Let's put this pie on the cooling rack, honey."

As Bertie lifted the fragrant pie from the oven and carried it to a small wire cooling rack on the other side of the kitchen, Jillian studied the young woman. Were the wisps escaping the careless blonde ponytail and the stains on her wrinkled white blouse a result of kitchen work, or was she unkempt by nature? Or was Jillian being too critical of someone doing what Jillian should have been doing all along?

"You said you laid aside your 'work' to help Bertie," she said to Kandi. "What is this work you do?"

Kandi straightened from inhaling the aroma of the pie and gestured toward a messy pile of notebooks, loose papers, and a laptop on the kitchen table.

"I'm a journalist."

"You're a reporter."

"A journalist, actually."

Apparently there was a difference, but right then, Jillian didn't care.

"Does my grandmother know?"

Kandi looked as if she'd been insulted. "Of course she knows."

"Kandi is the only one of them who acted with kindness or good raising," Bertie said. "She even offered to pitch in and help."

"But—"

Savannah came into the kitchen with an empty coffeepot and tea pitcher. "I came for refills."

"I have the drinks all ready for you," Kandi said. "I do hope the sweet tea is all right. I may have made it too sweet. Or not sweet enough."

Savannah smiled. "Don't worry about it."

Kandi took the empty coffeepot and the pitcher from her.

"I've arranged another plate of Bertie's nibbles, if you want to take it out. I'll bring you coffee and tea in a jiff."

"Thanks, Kandi." She sailed out the door with the plate.

"What about that tea cart?" Jillian asked of no one in particular.

"I'll bring it back to the kitchen after I finish filling cups and glasses." Kandi gave her a bright smile.

Jillian shook off an inclination to be irritable and went back to the other room. Why was Kandi Kerber, an utter stranger and a "journalist" to boot, acting as if she were Bertie's right hand? If she was after the facts, why didn't she ask like all the rest of them?

"Stop stewing. She's a bright spot for your grandmother today," Savannah said, pausing next to Jillian.

"So you're a mind reader now?"

"No. But I know you. Stop worrying. Having someone willing to help in a time of need is a blessing. At least Kandi is taking your grandmother's mind off dead bodies and police presence."

"She's a reporter. She'll be reminding Bertie about it soon enough, I imagine."

"Chill." Savannah handed the plate of crackers, cheese, olives, and tiny pickles to Jillian. "Hold this while I take the tea cart to the kitchen."

Jillian looked around the room. The Sweetie Pies were almost as intrusive as the reporters, but at least they were kindhearted friends who cared. It still seemed strange to her that Belle Haven's parlor was filled with smiling people while the sheriff's department was there because of a murder.

Creepy. That's what it is. Creepy.

By midafternoon, Jillian had shooed away a television crew and what she could only assume were a couple of journalism students from a nearby college. Concerned friends and neighbors eventually ceased to drop in, and once the deputies had left, the Sweetie Pies finally returned to their own homes or places of business, after receiving promises of updates as soon possible.

Coy Henderson remained, interviewing everyone who'd been in Belle Haven in the last forty-eight hours. Judging by the amount of time he kept each person in the library, Jillian figured he now knew everything from their first memory as a child to their favorite brand of ice cream. As soon as he had finished with one person and had sent them out, he barked the name of the next one to be interrogated.

Finally, he hollered for Jillian to return. He held up the bagged garden scissors. "So tell me about these."

If he'd been less astute, she might have suspected he'd forgotten about the scissors. But Henderson was shrewd, and she knew he'd saved the conversation for reasons she might never learn.

"Aunt Cornelia wanted to cut some gardenias this morning. I guess those are the scissors she was going to use."

"You guess?"

"She got some scissors out of the shed. But then, when we found Charmaine's body . . . Well, I don't know what happened to them. She must have dropped them."

"Hmm."

There was no way she was going to mention that Cornelia couldn't find the other pair of scissors she had searched for, the ones she couldn't remember where she'd left.

Surely she hadn't left them in Charmaine's body. Surely not.

Jillian did her best to keep her face completely impassive as she asked, "Did you ask Aunt Cornelia about those scissors?"

"I find it interesting that you did not say a word about them this morning when we first talked."

She bit her lip and remained silent. After all, if she said nothing, she couldn't blab anything incriminating against Cornelia.

Henderson drummed his fingers on the desktop. "Okay, Jillian. You can go."

His words surprised her so much, she could only blink at him.

"Go. But remember this: Anything you are hiding, I'll uncover."

"I know." Her voice broke.

"Go now."

Cornelia sat white-faced and silent in her chair, tatting as if she'd never do another thing in her life. She didn't even look out the window at the garden.

Jillian squatted next to her chair and leaned close. She glanced around and saw no one was near enough to hear if they kept their voices quiet.

"Aunt Cornelia," she whispered, "what did you tell the sheriff?"

The tatting shuttle moved at lightning speed. "Just what happened."

"Did you mention the garden scissors?"

Cornelia lifted her eyes, and Jillian read fear in them. "I told him I got a pair out of the shed and must have dropped them or something when we saw the poor dead body."

"Nothing else?"

"No. Why?" What little color was in her face suddenly drained, and her hands stilled. "Jillian, you didn't tell him I couldn't remember what I'd done with that other pair, did you?"

"No, ma'am. Not a word."

"Let's keep it that way, shall we?" She turned back to her silence and her tatting, leaving Jillian feeling slightly sick and off-balance. But she'd do whatever it took to protect her aunt. If that meant keeping her observations and opinions to herself, that's what she'd do.

It was a relief to her when the sheriff finally took his leave a short time later.

"Don't any of you leave Nathan County. You won't like the result if you try it." He stood in the living room and pinned a hard look on Jillian. "Make sure those two boys visiting y'all understand that."

One of those "two boys" had retreated to his room upstairs the moment he'd come out of the library, and the other, Jack Porter, now sat in the farthest corner of the living room that he could. He had been looking at the same magazine since he'd emerged from the library shortly after noon. He was staring at the sheriff, his expression inscrutable.

"I'll tell them," Jillian said, "but I'm sure they already know. Jack is staying at the Southern Peach Inn. I assume he's free to go back there now?"

Henderson's gaze went to him and nodded one time. "We'll be keeping an eye on *all* of y'all," he said to the room in general but looking at Jack.

Soon after the sheriff left, Bertie excused herself and headed to Moss Hollow to check on Lenora and the bakery.

Kandi Kerber, her notebook in hand, her laptop and other bulging notebooks on the floor nearby, sat on an ottoman next to Cornelia, seemingly enraptured by the lace the woman was making. Cornelia's pale cheeks had regained some of their color as she cheerfully chatted with Kandi. She showed her the tatting shuttle and explained about the thread.

"I'll show you how, if you'd like to learn," Jillian overheard her say.

"I'd love it. But first let me watch you for a while. I'll even take some notes." She opened her notebook and began writing without looking at the page. She focused hard on the work in Cornelia's hands.

"You certainly write fast," Jillian said after watching the pair for a bit. She glanced at the woman's collection of notebooks. "And a lot, apparently."

"Oh, I'm a trained notetaker," Kandi said, laughing a little. She pushed back a stray lock of hair. "And I write about everything."

"I see you have a laptop, but you seem to prefer to use notebooks."

"I like pen and paper best." She leaned forward and looked at the delicate design Cornelia had made. "Do you tat, Jillian?"

"Mercy, child," Cornelia said, "I would have taught her long ago if I thought she'd sit still long enough to learn."

"I embroider," Jillian said, somewhat defensively. "You have to sit still to embroider."

Kandi laughed. "My grandmother's favorite pastime is scuba diving." Both women looked at her in surprise. "She lives in Hawaii."

"Do you dive?" Cornelia's hands stopped.

"No, ma'am, not me. I don't like water. I like words. Now. Back to the story you were telling me about your grandfather and the catfish."

Jillian had heard the tale plenty of times, so she left the two alone. But she did wonder when Kandi was going to start asking questions about Charmaine's death. Although, looking at her great-aunt happily talking about her childhood and tatting with joy rather than desperation, and how much Bertie had relaxed in the young woman's presence, it seemed like having Kandi around was a blessing she'd failed to recognize. She couldn't help but wonder, though, how Bertie and Cornelia would feel when the young woman put down her pleasant side and picked up her journalist side. At least for now, with Kandi taking some of the pressure away from the twins, and Savannah helping to field calls and chase away unwanted visitors, the day would surely end more peacefully than it had begun.

"I'm going to go to town and see how Bertie and Lenora are doing," Jillian said to Savannah a little later. "Can you hold down the fort and keep an eye on . . ." She glanced at Cornelia.

"You betcha. Right now, she seems pretty content."

"Thanks, friend. I won't be long."

"Take as long as you need away from this place," Savannah said. "You might not be elderly, but this situation has been hard on you too. Give yourself a little breathing space."

She impulsively hugged Savannah. "There aren't many friends as good as you."

Savannah laughed as she returned the hug. "On the contrary. There are a lot of good friends in the world. You'd do the same for me if I were going through this, and you know it. Go now. You're leaving everything here in good hands."

At The Chocolate Shoppe, Jillian let herself in through the back door. Voices coming from upstairs let her know Lenora and Bertie were in Lenora's apartment.

Both women were sitting in the tiny, immaculate living room. Each cradled a cup of fragrant Earl Grey tea.

"What are you doing here, young'un?" Lenora asked. "Want a cup of tea?"

Before she could reply, Bertie sat up straight. Her tired face took on fresh lines of worry. "Is anything wrong at home?"

"No, no," Jillian said hurriedly. "I came to see if you two are all right. It's been such an upside-down day."

"We're fine," Lenora said. "I'm finer than your grandma, of course."

Bertie gave her friend a warm smile. "I caught this woman ladling up a pot of her good potato soup to bring to us," she said. "That's what she was doing instead of taking the rest of the day off like she was supposed to."

"Bless you to pieces, Lenora, but we have enough food at Belle Haven to feed three armies," Jillian said.

"That's what I told her, but—"

"I made it for y'all, and I want you to take it. I have a feeling this situation will take a few days to resolve. You're likely to have plenty of callers before it's all said and done. Offer them cookies and whatnot, but you girls need to eat my soup. Good for what ails you." She folded her arms and pursed her lips as if preparing for an argument, but no one in Jillian's acquaintance argued with Lenora when she looked like that.

"Thank you so much," Jillian said, smiling. "You're such a good friend."

"Absolutely," Bertie added.

"I don't mind a little excitement now and again," Jillian said, "but as far as I'm concerned, this has gone far past excitement."

"Coy Henderson knows what he's doing," Bertie said, and not for the first time. "Let's trust him and the process. And the good Lord, of course."

"I say amen to all that," Lenora added, nodding enthusiastically.

"It'll be business as usual at the bakery tomorrow," Bertie said, "but I need you to keep an eye on things at the house, Jillian. Cornelia especially needs some tending. She seems . . . well, not herself."

"I know."

Bertie nodded. "This excitement hasn't been good for her."

"If you want me stay home with her tomorrow, I will." She shifted her gaze to Lenora. "But you tell me ASAP if Bertie needs me back here at The Chocolate Shoppe. Promise?"

"I'll look after Bertie. You look after your great-aunt. And yes, honey, you can rest assured I'll call you if I need to."

Bertie stirred, her face settling into a thundercloud. "Talking about me as if I'm a kid, or worse, an infirm old woman. Both of you hush it right now. I'm perfectly fine."

"Of course you are," Jillian hastened to assure her. "But this situation with Charmaine's death has taken its toll on all of us."

Lenora fixed her stubborn dark-eyed gaze on Bertie. "Give this little gal permission to fuss and worry over you, for mercy's sake. You do enough fretting and fussing for twenty people your own self. She learned it from you."

"That's right," Jillian said, nodding enthusiastically.

Bertie sniffed. "Well." She took a noisy sip of her tea. "How was Cornelia when you left?"

"You saw her, talking to Kandi a mile a minute, telling old family tales, I think. And I believe she's going to teach her to tat."

Bertie turned to Lenora. "That little girl walked into the house, and it was like a breath of fresh air. She looked around, saw how busy and chaotic everything was, and said to me, 'Let me help you. The story can wait.' And she jumped right in."

"But you still don't really know her, Bertie," Jillian said. "How do you know she's not going to claim she's descended from Captain Hoyt's fourth wife?"

Bertie looked as if she didn't know whether to frown or laugh. She waved one hand.

"You need to give that girl the benefit of the doubt." Lenora spoke with such firmness that Jillian knew the two had already discussed Kandi.

"She does seem very kind and helpful," Jillian admitted.

"And not sneaky." Bertie shot a glance at Lenora. "I hate to speak ill of the dead, but that Charmaine seemed sneaky, always eyeing things in the house like she was up to no good."

"And phony, from what I saw," Lenora added, nodding. "If that girl was from the South, I'm the Flying Nun. So what do you think Charmaine was looking for?"

"She never seemed very interested in anything she saw. For all her talk about family history, she barely gave those portraits upstairs a passing glance." Jillian said, "I think she was looking for something else. Something in particular. She was interested in looking in the attic and in the cellar, and oddly enough, that old chest of drawers in my bedroom seemed of special interest to her."

"What?" Lenora's face was a mask of outrage. "You telling me she wanted your nighties and socks and undies and T-shirts?"

"I haven't got a clue, but I bet Bryce knows exactly what she wanted."

Bertie sat up straight. "I bet he does too. How could he not? But getting that boy to talk is like pulling teeth from a rock."

"Close-mouthed, is he?" Lenora asked.

"And how!" Jillian nodded. "But guess what?"

"Oh, lookee there, Bertie. Look at that smile. She's got a plan. What's your plan, sugar?"

Jillian leaned toward them and lowered her voice. "He likes Savannah. Maybe he'll tell her."

Bertie looked less than impressed. "Soon?" she asked.

"Tonight at dinner, if we can get him out of his room. If not, then maybe she can talk to him privately."

Bertie glowered at Jillian, scandalized. "I'm not throwing that girl into his room, just the two of them. No, sir."

"That's not what I meant, and you know it. I'm not sure yet how we'll work it out, but leave it to me and Savannah."

Jillian started to drive back to Belle Haven, but she craved a bit of quiet time away from the dark aura that surrounded Belle Haven right then. She needed some peace and quiet, an opportunity to let her mind rest.

She drove to the nearby park and strolled along the soft, newly clipped grass until she settled on a bench that overlooked a lily garden. A mockingbird sang nearby, and a couple of squirrels chittered in the trees. A cool, fragrant breeze caressed her face. She closed her eyes and tried to lose herself in the still beauty of nature around her, but thoughts of recent events crowded out any hard-won peace of mind. Unanswered questions scrolled through her brain in double-time, like a musical roll from an old player piano.

What, if anything, had been written on that scrap of paper in Charmaine's hand?

Is there any trace evidence left on it?

Had Aunt Cornelia resented Charmaine for more reasons than the brief animosity between Possum and Dipsy Doodle? And what kind of reason is that to kill someone?

Besides, could she have killed the much younger, much stouter woman? If she did, could it be deemed a crime of passion?

If she goes to prison, will she be treated with kindness?

Jillian's eyes flew open, and she sat straight up on the bench. *How stupid can I be to suspect Aunt Cornelia, even for a millisecond?*

Her phone rang, and she pulled it from her pocket.

"Jillian," Bertie's voice greeted her, "I don't know where you are or what you're doing, but come home right now. Cornelia has had another fainting spell, and we have another unexpected guest. I need you here. *Now.*"

Jillian had no idea how time had passed so quickly. When she had settled on the park bench, the sun was still above the western horizon, but inky shadows were beginning to fall from trees and houses as she drove back to Belle Haven.

"Jillian," Kandi said the moment she walked in the door, "I'm so glad you're home. Cornelia has locked herself in her room, and she won't let anyone in but me, not even the doctor. I'm taking her this cup of tea." She held up a full blue-and-white china cup on a saucer. "Your grandmother is upset. She's upstairs with Dr. Taylor, and I'm unsure what to do about anything."

Jillian felt an unexpected flood of warmth toward the young woman. Kandi's blue eyes looked ready to brim with tears, her face full of worry. Jillian touched her shoulder briefly.

"Thank you for your concern. Where's Savannah?"

"She left before all this happened. I guess she went home."

"I see. Tell me what happened."

Kandi glanced at her watch. "About thirty minutes ago, this fellow showed up at the door. Said his name was Arthur Fremont and that he was here to see Cornelia."

Jillian frowned. "I've heard that name before."

"I was the one who answered the door, so I took him into the living room where Aunt Cornelia was. She took one look at him, stood up, then fell over in a dead faint."

"Where is he now, this man?"

"In the living room. He's sitting there like a stone. Jillian, what should I do?"

"Here." She handed Kandi her cell phone and took the tea.

"I'll take this up. You call Savannah and tell her to get over here."

"No police, right?"

"I don't see how the law can help in this situation. Call Savannah, then offer that new fellow some tea or coffee. Something to keep him occupied until I get back. Okay?"

"Gotcha."

Jillian hurried up the stairs. Her grandmother paced back and forth in front of Cornelia's bedroom door. In a well-tailored dark-blue suit, the tall, gray-haired family physician stood patiently to one side. Dr. John Taylor was nearing his seventieth birthday, but he was as lean and fit now as he had been when Jillian was young. The kindness in his blue eyes underscored his mild-mannered demeanor.

"See if you can get her to unlock this," Bertie said. "Maybe she'll listen to you. Or to Kandi. She's taken quite a shine to that little girl." She glanced down the corridor. "I thought she was bringing Cornelia some tea."

"I have the tea, and Kandi is calling Savannah." She looked at the doctor. "Do you think she's okay, Dr. Taylor?"

"It's hard to say since she won't let me see her," Dr. Taylor said. "She sounds fine when she talks to us, but she's determined not to come out or let anyone in, except her new friend. I understand this is her second fainting episode in four days. I want to make sure she's all right."

Jillian tapped on the door. "Aunt Cornelia, it's Jillian. Can you hear me?"

"I'm not deaf." Cornelia's voice was strong and clear.

"I have your tea."

Silence. Then, "Kandi is bringing me tea."

Jillian looked at her grandmother, who lifted her brows and shrugged.

"Kandi is doing something else for a minute. Would you let me come inside?"

"There's no purpose to it. I'll wait for Kandi. She understands."

"Understands what?"

Silence.

"At least let me give it to you before it gets cold."

Silence.

"Let me see what I can do," Dr. Taylor said. He straightened his shoulders as if about to face an adversary and thumped on the door. "Cornelia Montgomery, as your doctor, I demand to come in and at least take your blood pressure."

Jillian had never heard him raise his voice or speak so sternly.

"John Taylor, I told you a dozen times already that I am perfectly fine."

"Then prove it by letting me check your vitals." He rattled the locked doorknob.

"I'm back," Kandi said, hurrying toward them. "I called Savannah, and she'll be here soon. And that man who was downstairs earlier? He's gone."

"Gone?"

"He just up and walked out while I was calling Savannah."

"How peculiar!" Bertie's frown deepened. "What did he say?"

"Nothing. Maybe he realized his presence was a problem."

"Who *is* he?" Jillian asked. "Why was he here?"

Bertie lifted both hands. "I don't know. He said he knew Cornelia and wanted to reconnect with her. But let me tell you something." She pointed a finger at Jillian to make her point. "She obviously knows him, and it's even more apparent she doesn't want to see him. If he knows her as well as he seems to think he does, then he should know she's as stubborn as five Missouri mules. She'll hole up in her room for a month of Sundays."

"You think he'll come back?" Jillian asked.

"Maybe not," Kandi said. "He seemed pretty discouraged. Anyway, I think Aunt Cornelia will come out now." She rapped on the door. "Aunt Cornelia? It's Kandi. Arthur Fremont left a few minutes ago."

Silence. "Are you sure?"

"Yes, ma'am. He's gone, and so is his car."

The door opened a crack. One blue eye regarded the worried quartet. "Is he coming back?"

"I don't know. I hope not."

"Aunt Cornelia," Jillian said, "we won't let him back in the house since he upsets you so much, so at least come down and have a nice supper."

"Yes, do that," Dr. Taylor said. "If you don't, I may be forced to take you to the hospital."

His words hung in the air with all the joy of an approaching heat wave. Cornelia stared at him through the crack in the door for a good twenty seconds, then finally heaved a sigh.

"All right. But you people get away from this door. Do not hover. I'm no invalid; I want my privacy. Kandi, honey, come on in here and bring my tea. You can walk me downstairs in a minute."

She smiled fondly at Kandi and patted her back as the young woman took the tea from Jillian and slipped inside the room. Why did Cornelia want this girl, whom she barely knew, to be with her instead of her very own great-niece? Jillian tried hard to ignore a pang somewhere in the center of her chest.

"Let's go warm up some of that food, Jillian," Bertie said, turning away. "There's plenty of it, John, and you're more than welcome to stay for a bite to eat."

He glanced at his watch as they walked away together, talking quietly.

Jillian glanced down the hallway at Bryce's door. She hadn't seen him since he'd fled from the library earlier in the day. She wasn't sure whether she trusted the man or suspected him, but her conscience dictated that she should treat him with kindness.

She knocked on his door. Dipsy Doodle whimpered and snuffled at the door.

"Bryce, we're going to be sitting down to supper soon," she said through the closed door. "Would you like to join us?"

She heard a soft stirring, and a few moments later, he opened the door, yawning and blinking. His brown hair was mussed, and he had a pillow crease on his cheek. With his shirttail untucked, slacks wrinkled, and feet bare, he hardly resembled himself.

"I'm so sorry to wake you," she said.

"That's all right. I need to take Dipsy Dee out, anyway." He looked down at the little dog, who was wagging her tail and licking Jillian's shoe.

"We'll be having supper soon. It'll be potluck from all that food people brought over today."

"That's all right with me. I'm not picky." His smile was so warm, so friendly, that it transformed his face completely.

She took a step back and tried to hide her surprise. "I'm going to go help lay out the food. We'll probably eat in about half an hour or so."

"All right. Thanks, Jillian. I'll take the dog out, then come back and freshen up for dinner." He gave her another smile, then closed the door between them.

Bryce had seemed different, and it wasn't because he was rumpled from a nap. She thought about this all the way to the kitchen.

"Bertie," she said, kissing one of her grandmother's soft cheeks, "I'll store the food and tidy everything away after supper, so promise me you'll go to bed early tonight. In fact, why don't you sit down right over there at the table and put your feet up—"

Bertie made a noise and flapped one hand dismissively. "I'm fine. I had a nice little rest when I was at Lenora's. Now, then." She tied her apron and opened the refrigerator. "We have so much food, let's warm up what is best served warm and set everything else out. We'll serve it buffet style."

Jillian knew Bertie would work doggedly until she made up her mind to stop. The best Jillian could do was take on as much of that work as she possibly could. With the kitchen table full of covered dishes and casseroles, she set the table in the dining room. The memory of Charmaine using the best linen and china, lighting candles, and putting on a display equal to a holiday celebration was fresh in her mind, and it stung. If only she'd known that soon the woman would be dead, Jillian might have had more patience with her and tried to have understood her a little better.

Charmaine had been irritating and off-putting, but she hadn't deserved her fate. No one deserved that.

The doorbell interrupted her work. Somehow, seeing Jack Porter on the doorstep failed to surprise her.

"Hi, Jack." She wondered if her voice betrayed the weariness she felt.

"Hello, Jillian." He shifted from foot to foot and failed to meet her eyes. "I'm a little embarrassed."

"Why's that?"

He ran a hand through his thinning hair and shot a swift, self-conscious glance at her.

"When I came here to get Charmaine, I thought she'd come back home with me right away. I didn't expect her to stay here. I sure didn't expect her to get . . ." He ducked his head. "Well, you know."

"I don't think many of us expected that."

He cleared his throat and ducked his head even more. Jillian wondered briefly if he was trying to hide his face so she couldn't read his eyes, or if he truly was embarrassed.

"The thing is, I'm in a bind. I had enough money to fly back home. I didn't expect to spend a couple of nights in a hotel or to rent a car. Honestly, I don't have funds to buy meals while I'm here. I've barely got enough to get back to Charlottesville." He shifted his weight from foot to foot. "If you could give me a bite to eat while I'm here, until the sheriff says it's okay for me to go home, I'd be beholden to you." He finally lifted his head. "I'll send you a check, as soon as I get paid. I have a job at Findlay Ford in Baker Creek. You can call and ask them. I'm good for it, as long as I can get back there by Monday."

Jillian bit her lip and studied him. His face darkened, and she thought she saw the shimmer of tears.

"We're not going to let you go hungry, Jack. Come on in."

Relief filled his face. "Thank you, Jillian."

"Have a seat in the living room. We'll be eating directly." She went into the kitchen. "Bertie, I'm laying another place for supper."

Bertie pulled a pan of rolls from the oven. She looked over the wave of heat that danced between them. "Who else is coming besides Savannah?"

"Jack."

Bertie frowned. "Charmaine's boyfriend?"

Jillian nodded. "He wasn't prepared to be away from home this long."

"Never mind. Doesn't matter, as long as the two men get along. You know, last week in Sunday school class, we talked about hospitality. I was all for it." She met Jillian's eyes and laughed a little. "Not so sure I'll be as enthusiastic if that lesson is revisited this coming Sunday." She glanced around at the food. "It's ready, honey. Why don't you call the others to the table. Oh, and, Jillian?"

"Yes, ma'am?"

Bertie looked at her for a moment, then drew her into an embrace. "I don't say it often enough, honey, but I do love you. So very much. I'm not sure how Cornelia and I ever got along without you."

"Oh my," Jillian squeaked. Her grandmother was a warm, loving woman, but displays of affection were rare. She hugged Bertie as tightly as she dared. "I love you too."

Bertie stepped back, patted Jillian's cheek as if she were tiny, then said, "Get the others and we'll eat."

Jillian hardly recognized Bryce when he came downstairs. Dressed casually in jeans and a long-sleeved, button-down, pale-green shirt and his hair combed rather than styled, he seemed younger, fitter, and even a bit taller. His eyes had lost the dogged look of someone always on edge and had taken on a warmer expression, as if he would rather be friendly than aloof. He looked cheerful and refreshed. It was highly possible, even likely, that he had not experienced grief as much as shock. Now that reality had set in, maybe he had reached a point of relief.

Dipsy Doodle followed him but stopped in the doorway of the dining room. The small ears pricked forward, then back, the fluffy tail dropped from its curled position over her back and hung lankly behind her. She gave a little growl, then a little cry.

"Come on, Dipsy Dee," Bryce said, looking at her. "I'll give you a bit of chicken."

"Why, look at how she's shivering," Jillian said. "That's what she was doing this morning when I found her."

"Poor little thing," Kandi said, her expression concerned. She went to Dipsy Doodle and reached out to pet her. The dog bared her teeth and raised her hackles. "Oh my," she said, drawing back her hand quickly.

"She's never done that to anyone before," Bryce said, "but she's been pretty traumatized. I'll take her upstairs." He scooped up the dog, and she cowered against him, whimpering. He glanced around the room. "Maybe she's afraid of the cat again. Is Possum in here?"

"Possum is under my bed," Cornelia said. "At least he was.

He knows when things upset me, so if he's not on the bed, he's under it. Besides, that dog and Possum made up their differences."

"Well, whatever the cause, I'll take her upstairs and be right back. Excuse me."

"Poor little dog," Kandi said again as she sat down. "I hate it when animals suffer, don't you?" The others agreed and chatted quietly, waiting for Bryce to return before eating.

The meal was tasty and plentiful, but with Charmaine's murder hanging in the air like an unpleasant odor, the mood was subdued. Kandi's presence was a gentle, nearly invisible one of servitude as she kept an eye on everyone's plates and glasses, making sure they had what they needed. She especially watched over the twins.

Jillian tried to be grateful, but somewhere back in the far corner of her heart, petty jealousy stirred and would not be quieted. In fact, the niggling little notion that Kandi was trying to take her place wormed its way right into her brain.

I'm being foolish, she told herself more than once. *I should be glad to have someone around so willing to help. Besides, she'll be gone soon enough.*

"I'm unsure if this is the right time and place to ask," Kandi said at one point, "and I hate to bring it up at the dinner table, but this has been the first chance I've had to talk with everyone. Not that I begrudge the time I've spent helping Grandma Bertie and Aunt Cornelia. I've loved doing that." She paused to bestow a warm smile on them.

Jillian yearned to take a napkin and wipe the smear of butter off the girl's chin. Instead, she smiled. "Bertie hates to be called Grandma."

Kandi smiled brighter than ever. "Okay. Then I'll call her Mammaw."

"She doesn't like Mammaw either. Or Nana, or Mimi, or MeeMaw, or Grandmother, or Granny." She felt a twinge of guilty pleasure when some of Kandi's proprietary light-beam dimmed. She decided to change the subject before Bertie did the unthinkable and gave Kandi permission to call her something Jillian had always been forbidden to say. "I thought reporters had to get the stories quickly. Deadlines and all that."

Kandi squirmed a little. "Yes, well, that's true. But my newspaper is very small and doesn't come out every day or anything. Besides, my blog's the thing."

Jillian's eyebrows went up. "Your *blog*? You're writing about this murder on your blog?"

Kandi nodded enthusiastically and opened the notebook she always kept with her. She picked up her pen.

"You need to eat, honey," Cornelia said to her. "Put away your pen and paper for now."

"Yes," Bertie said, "we can talk later."

"Oh, no," Kandi said brightly. "I can write and eat at the same time. I do it all the time. Besides, my subscribers are waiting." Her smile included everyone. "So, please tell me about what happened here earlier. That woman, how she died, why she was here."

For someone who hated to bring up the topic at dinner, she seemed to have no qualms pursuing the gruesome subject.

"Bryce and Jack, you were the closest to Charmaine," Jillian said. "It's understandable if you'd rather not be present while Kandi gets her story, and if so, she can do it after dinner."

There was a brief pause before Bryce spoke. "Feel free to ask questions. It's okay."

"Sure." Jack shrugged. "I got nothing to hide. Or to lose. Go for it."

"Goody!" Kandi said, almost giggling in excitement.

No one said anything, waiting for her questions. When she simply sat, pen poised above the paper, Savannah came to the rescue.

"Well," she said as she laid down her fork, "her name, as I'm sure you know by now, was Charmaine Rawlins. Apparently she was a distant relative. Right?"

"She *said* she was a relative," Cornelia said, "but I'm not so sure about that."

Kandi ate a bite of potato pancake and wrote in her notebook. She looked at Bryce. "You knew her better than anyone here. Was she a relative?" she asked.

He shifted in his chair, his brows drawn together. "I was only her personal assistant."

"But surely, if you were together a lot—"

"Practically joined at the hip," Jack muttered.

Bryce ignored him and said, "I only know what Charmaine told me, and most of that were demands for this or that."

Bertie pointed her chin at Jillian. "You were looking for information to back up her claims. Tell Kandi about that."

Jillian did not want to assassinate the dead woman's character, especially on someone's blog. "I found nothing."

Kandi's hand flew across the page, her face a study of concern and concentration. "Nothing. As in nothing to substantiate her claim to the Belle family name?"

"Right."

"Oh dear."

"Why does that distress you?" Savannah asked, leaning forward to look at her.

"I'm not exactly distressed. But don't you think it's sad she came here, apparently to connect with her family, but then you found nothing to prove her claim? And I find it sad that you felt you had to investigate her."

"We could hardly take her word for it, dear," Cornelia said. "After all, she was a complete stranger. I'm sure you understand."

"But *we're* complete strangers," Jack said to her, indicating himself, Bryce, and Kandi. "All three of us. Are you investigating us too?"

"None of you three sailed in here, making claims to the family," Bertie said. "I'm sure Charmaine was after something in particular, something beyond being part of the Belle family, but the thing is, we really have nothing of value anymore. So much was sold off long ago, and what is left is pretty much what you see here."

"She snooped around a lot," Cornelia added, "but she found nothing because there is nothing to find."

"Really?" Kandi's frown nearly caused her eyebrows to meet. "What was she looking for?"

"She never told me," Jack said. "She was too mad at me for finding her. But I bet she told him." He pointed at Bryce, and everyone looked at him. "I bet he knows a lot more than he's told anyone, including the sheriff."

Bryce's face reddened, and for a moment, Jillian thought he would explode with anger. Instead, he shifted in his chair a few times, then cleared his throat. He glanced at Kandi, at her hand over the notebook.

"She was looking for some documents," he said, meeting Bertie's eyes.

"Documents? Like a deed to Belle Haven or other properties?" Savannah asked.

"No. She was looking for certain letters."

"Letters?" Jillian echoed. "Old letters the family wrote to one another?"

He drew in a deep breath and blew it out, as if reluctant to share what he knew. "She was looking for the letters exchanged between Abraham Lincoln and John Wilkes Booth."

"*What?*" Bertie, Cornelia, and Jillian yelped at the same time.

"Apparently, according to these letters, Lincoln had hired Booth as a spy—for the *South*, to ensure the North would lose."

"WHAT?" they all yelled again, this time with Jack and Savannah joining in.

"That's the craziest thing I've ever heard," Savannah said.

"It certainly is," Bertie said. "Where in the world did she get a notion like that?"

He leaned forward. "You mean you've never heard of these letters?"

Kandi scribbled furiously, her eyes going from face to face so fast, it made Jillian's head swim.

"Never!" Cornelia scowled at Bryce as if he'd been caught looking for the letters in her pajama drawer.

"There is no such thing," Bertie said firmly. "If there had been, they would have been turned over to a museum or government agency long ago. Why, the whole of history of the War Between the States would have to be rewritten."

"A person would have to be nuttier than twelve Christmas fruitcakes to believe something like that," Cornelia declared. "I hope *you* didn't believe it."

"I did what I was told," he said mildly and sat back.

"I'd like to know how Charmaine came by this information," Jillian said. "Who told her we had these letters at Belle Haven?"

Bryce spread his hands helplessly. "Arthur Fremont. He said Cornelia had told him about the correspondence long ago and that the family still had possession of all of it but had hidden it away."

"Arthur Fremont!" Cornelia said. "That awful man has crept out of my past like the evil snake in the grass that he is. He is a liar. He'd tell a lie when the truth would serve him better. There are no such letters."

"No indeed," Bertie chimed in. "And never have been."

This news flabbergasted Jillian, and how her great-aunt had come to know someone who upset her as much as this Arthur Fremont did was something she'd get to the bottom of, sooner or later. For now, though, she needed to make sure Cornelia's well-being and peace of mind took precedence.

"Don't get yourself in a tizzy, Aunt Cornelia," she said. "He's gone."

"Let's hope he's gone for good," Cornelia muttered, dabbing at her pale face with a napkin.

"Well, that explains why Charmaine was here," Savannah said, "but it doesn't explain why she was killed."

"Thank goodness Coy Henderson is on the job," Bertie said.

"Amen!" Cornelia added.

If dinner hadn't lost its appeal before, it certainly had by then.

Jack shifted in his chair. He ran his hands through his hair and coughed a couple of times.

"I guess now's the time for me to come completely clean too," he said. "You folks have been good to me." He shot a self-conscious look around the table. "I think you should know why I really followed Charmaine down here."

Everyone looked at him except Kandi, who was frowning hard at her notes as if she couldn't read them.

"It's really no big secret," Jack said, "but kinda embarrassing." He paused for so long, it seemed he'd changed his mind.

"Go on," Bertie said. "You'll feel better if you get everything off your chest."

"Yes, spit it out, for goodness' sake," Cornelia muttered.

"Aunt Cornelia," Jillian admonished gently, "be gracious." How often had Cornelia or Bertie said the same thing to her when she was exasperated?

Jack shifted in his chair again. "You know we were engaged, Charmaine and I. I don't know how or why, but she got it into her head that I owned a big Ford dealership in Charlottesville instead of working as a mechanic at a small dealership in Baker Creek." He twitched a little and avoided everyone's eyes. "Charmie was so pretty and elegant and classy that, well, I let her believe I had plenty of money. I did everything I could to keep up that appearance, spending all my paychecks to take her out and buy her things." He ran one hand over his thinning hair. "It was a whirlwind romance. I cleaned out every penny of my savings to buy her the biggest, brightest, flashiest diamond ring I could find in town." He passed around another uncomfortable glance.

"Oh, what a tangled web we weave," Cornelia intoned, gazing at him through narrowed eyes. "She found out you were broke, didn't she?"

"Yes, ma'am. About four days after we got engaged. You can't fool people forever. I know that. But if I'd been straight with her from the very first, we'd never have been together at all. Once she knew the truth, we had a big fight. Well, I mostly just dodged words and everything else she threw at me. She wouldn't listen when I told her how much I loved her and how I'd do anything for her and how money doesn't make a marriage, love does."

Bryce snorted and looked amused. "Jack, you didn't know the real Charmaine *at all*. If you had, you would have saved yourself the trip down here."

Jack glared at him. "Oh yeah? Well, I had to try one last time. And since she wouldn't listen to me, I wanted to get that ring back. I need the money I invested in that thing."

"And did she give it back to you?" Savannah asked.

"No. If she had, I would've gone straight back to Baker Creek." He pointed at Bryce. "He probably has it. Got it hidden somewhere."

"Don't be stupid," Bryce growled. "I imagine she either sold it the minute she broke up with you, or it's in the bank vault."

Jack sagged in his chair. "Man, I have bills to pay. I'm going to lose everything because of her."

"Sounds like a perfect motive for murder to me," Kandi said, looking up from her notes.

Dead silence fell while everyone looked at her.

"No way!" he shouted at her, glaring. Then he lowered his voice and spoke to the others. "And just so you know, I told the sheriff all of this. I'm waiting for him to give me the go ahead to leave Moss Hollow. I thought I should let you know the full truth about me. I feel as if I owe y'all that much."

"Thank you for that," Jillian said. She wasn't sure she believed him completely, but what he said made sense.

"Yes, thank you, Jack," Bertie said. "Now, anyone want more hot rolls? There are plenty more in the bun warmer." She got halfway out of her chair.

"Sit down, Bertie," Cornelia fussed. "If anyone wants another roll, we all know where they are."

Kandi tapped her pen against her notebook, turned to a fresh page, and passed around a glance to each person at the table. "The lede for my story needs to be about the murder. I came in a little late, you know. Grandma Bertie and I have mostly talked about cooking and baking." She turned a smile to Cornelia. "And Aunt Cornelia and I have talked about everything except Charmaine's death. So now, I need to get down to business and get my story written. Someone tell me, please, what have the police done? What have they told you?"

"It's the sheriff's department, dear, not the police," Cornelia corrected, "and our sheriff is very close-mouthed."

"I think we'll find out she was killed with a pair of garden scissors," Bertie said.

Cornelia, who was drinking water, dropped the glass onto her plate, breaking both. Kandi, who had a mouthful of potato salad, choked on it. Her pen and notebook fell to the floor.

"Oh my," Bertie said. Everyone went into a state of activity, fumbling for napkins, pounding Kandi's back, retrieving broken glass, grabbing her notebook and shaking food off of it.

"Excuse me," Kandi managed to croak. She pointed at Cornelia. "When she said scissors . . . then Aunt Cornelia dropped her glass, it startled me."

"Those scissors . . . They can't prove a thing." Cornelia sat, white-faced, staring at them before she passed out for yet the third time.

19

Jillian woke with a stiff neck that turned into a full-blown headache the moment she opened her eyes.

Sleeping in a hard, vinyl chair in a hospital room was low on her list of favorite things to do, but right then, she didn't care where she'd spent the night or if her head felt as though someone had put it in a hay baler. Cornelia slept soundly in a narrow bed with machines hooked to her. Daylight filtered through half-closed metal blinds and threw slanted shadows across a room that wrapped them in calm, soft shades of blue.

"Did she rest all right?" Savannah's stage whisper from near the doorway startled Jillian so badly she jumped. "I'm sorry. I should have knocked, but I didn't want to wake her if she was asleep."

Jillian stood and stretched the painful kinks from her neck, back, and legs. "They gave her a pill, and right now, I don't think a thunderstorm during a fireworks display would disturb her."

Savannah held out a huge cup of coffee from one of the coffee shops nearby. "I figured the vending machine brew wasn't the thing for you this morning."

"Bless you. Just what I need. Thank you." Jillian barely blew on it before she sipped.

Savannah walked over to the bed and gazed down at the sleeping woman. She picked up one hand and stroked it.

"Poor dear," she murmured, bending over to kiss Cornelia's forehead. "Do they know why she's been fainting?"

"She's anemic and her blood pressure is low. Dr. Taylor is going to run a few other tests on her, so he's keeping her a day or two—more if necessary."

Jillian and Savannah stood on opposite sides of the bed, gazing down. The machines beeped and flashed in a way that caused Jillian's head to throb even worse.

"I look at her like this, and I can't help but think . . ." She gulped. "What if there's something really wrong with her? I've always taken it for granted that she and Bertie will always be here. What if . . ." Her voice broke.

Savannah reached across the bed and grabbed her hand. "Those two women might be old, but, honey, they are *strong*. In every way you can imagine they have strength. You have it too." She squeezed Jillian's fingers, hard. "Keep your chin up and keep going, no matter what. That's what Bertie and Cornelia do." She glanced at Cornelia and smiled. "Of course, there are times when you should slow down a bit and take care of yourself."

Jillian sniffled and reached for the small box of the thin, rough tissues the hospital provided. She wiped her eyes and blinked hard, forcing herself to swallow back depressing thoughts.

"I know," she choked out. "You're right. You're always right, Savannah. That's why I rely on you so much."

"Yes, honey. I am definitely perfect."

"I didn't say that."

"No, but that's what you meant. Right?"

They looked at each other and giggled like they did when they were girls. It felt good to laugh, even though Jillian had no idea what the next few days were going to bring.

Savannah's smile faded, and she tipped her head to one side. She ran her gaze over to Jillian, then looked into her eyes. "This week has been rough on you. You are completely stressed out."

"It's been rough on all of us." Jillian pulled in a deep breath. "I'm worried as much about Bertie as I am Cornelia. She was here until after midnight and back again at four this morning. She tried to send me home too. She finally gave in when I refused for the fiftieth time. So you know what she did? She went to The Chocolate Shoppe."

"That sounds like her."

"I know. I'm afraid she's going to end up in here too." Her voice broke.

Savannah reached out and touched her arm. "Listen, don't let yourself start thinking that way. Don't let those thoughts take hold. Hear me?"

Jillian heard her, and she understood the comfort her friend offered, but all the kind words in the world could not erase her worry.

"I'm here now, and I don't have any plans," Savannah continued. "Why don't you run home, get a shower, and freshen up? Get yourself a bite to eat, maybe even take a walk or something. You'll feel better."

"But you've—"

"No use arguing, Jillian." She sat down and took a sip of her coffee. "I'm going to stay right here for a while. Go on now. Cornelia is in the best of hands, and I'll be here when you get back, I promise. In fact, I'll wager by the time you get back, she'll be awake, sitting up and sassier than ever."

Careful not to spill coffee all over either of them, Jillian gave her best friend a huge hug.

"I owe you."

"No, you don't. Friends don't owe each other anything, not in a case like this." Savannah got up, escorted Jillian to the door, and gave her gentle push. "Now go. Check on Bertie and take care of *you*."

"I'm not going home," Bertie said, punching down the dough for her famous Fun Buns, "and you can't make me."

The buns were made from a tricky recipe and took a long time to make. So far, the only one who'd ever been able to create Fun Buns that tasted right and had the preferred texture was Bertie. Jillian didn't know why her grandmother had chosen that day of all days to tackle Fun Buns.

"In fact," Bertie said, "I'm not going anywhere except to see my sister as soon as I close the bakery."

Jillian thought maybe Bertie had chosen to make the sturdy dough because it gave her an outlet upon which to vent her frustrations.

"She means it," Lenora said, meeting Jillian's eyes. "I've tried all morning to send her home. She's worn to a frazzle, but she won't go."

Her grandmother was determined to keep working, even when she was clearly weary.

Bertie paused in her work to run a gaze along Jillian's length. "You could use some freshening up. We're fine here. Maggie's helping."

"I suppose the sheriff or someone from his office has been in touch?"

"Not with me." Bertie paused for a moment, glaring down at the dough. "I may pop over to see him before I go home."

"Or I can go right now."

Bertie shook her head. "No. He's apt to be more open with me than you. You're still a kid in his eyes. I'm a mother figure."

"She goes all Freudian on us once in a while," Lenora said.

Jillian crimped her lips. "Sometimes Coy Henderson acts like his mother was a grizzly bear."

"You be nice," Bertie retorted immediately. "And go home now." She grabbed a fistful of paper towels and wiped her hands, then pulled Jillian into her arms. "Thank you, Jillian."

"For what?" The hug surprised her, but she returned it.

"Just for being you. I don't know what I'd do without you, honey. Take care of yourself, promise?"

"Of course."

Lenora stood behind Bertie, smiling and nodding.

"But you have to promise to do the same," Jillian added.

Bertie pulled away and patted her face. "I'm doing my best. Now, you get on home and check on Bryce and Dipsy Doodle. Jack will probably be there. Take some of those bear claws from the display for them. An old grizzly bear made them this morning."

Jillian had just boxed up eight bear claws when the bell above the door rang. She looked up to see Jack Porter enter the bakery.

"I need to talk to you and Miss Bertie," he said.

"Oh?" Was he getting ready to confess to something? Maybe he was going to ask for a loan.

She led him to the steamy, fragrant kitchen where her grand-mother was pinching the Fun Buns into gobs the size of golf balls. Lenora was on the far end of the room, wiping down equipment.

"Bertie, Jack has something he wants to talk to us about."

"What's going on?" She wiped her hands on her apron.

"I have three things to share with you," he said. "First, the sheriff came out to Belle Haven about thirty minutes ago." He paused to let that sink in, which Jillian found a little irritating. "Second, I'm on my way out of town. Henderson just cleared me." He grinned at both of them.

Bertie and Jillian exchanged looks, then Bertie said, "Good for you!"

"That's wonderful, Jack," Jillian said, smiling at him.

"Thank you." Once more he paused, as if for impact. "The third thing I have to tell you . . . he took Bryce in."

Both women gaped at him.

"What do you mean, he took Bryce in?" Bertie asked. "Arrested him?"

"I guess so. The sheriff told me I could go, and the next thing I know, the deputy is taking Bryce out of the house and putting him in the cruiser."

Jillian and Bertie stared at him.

"Forevermore," Bertie said faintly, clutching Jillian's arm.

Lenora came up behind them. "Shut my mouth! Y'all have been giving room and board to a murderer?"

Jillian could hardly believe it. But it made sense, especially considering the way Charmaine had bullied and abused the man. Jillian had sensed something more in Bryce, though. She was pretty sure he was a good man caught in a web he didn't know how to escape.

"Well, I can't say I'm surprised," Bertie said. "There was something about him . . . I knew it."

Jillian had no voice. She had actually *liked* Bryce Bellingham.

"What about Dipsy Doodle?" she asked when she could speak.

"One of the other deputies had her."

"Oh, not that awful Tina Bogle, I hope," Bertie said.

"No, ma'am. Not her."

Jack reached into the pocket of his rumpled jacket and pulled out a creased envelope. "Kandi left this for you, Miss Bertie. It was on the kitchen table when I got there. I guess she left really early."

"Kandi's *gone*?" Bertie took the envelope from him.

"Looks that way, ma'am. At least, she wasn't in Belle Haven while I was there."

"Oh my." Disappointment colored Bertie's voice as she unfolded the single page. She squinted, read it, and then passed it to Jillian. "Bless her heart. She must have written it like she writes everything else, without even looking at the page."

Thank you for your hospitalty. I beleive I have enough to write a nice little story. Love, Kandi.

"Hospitalty"? "Beleive"? Jillian told herself this was not the time to comment on the young woman's lack of spelling prowess.

Jack stuck out his right hand. "Well, Miss Bertie, Jillian. I need to get on the road." He shook hands with both of them. "Thanks again for your kindness to me . . . and to Charmie while she was with you. I wish we could have met under better circumstances."

After he left, the three women stood in silence, looking at each other.

"Well," Jillian said finally, "at least the house will be quiet when I get home."

"All the better for you to relax," Bertie said.

"And you too?"

"Nope. I'm finishing these buns, then I'm going to see my sister."

Belle Haven was more than quiet. It was eerie. Rather than finding the unaccustomed solitude relaxing, Jillian found it creepy. She kept imagining the image of Charmaine's cold, dead body, so she pulled the drapes to close off the view of the back garden. Even the sunshine falling through the stained glass dome failed to give her home a warm feeling of safety.

She took a couple of aspirin, had a quick shower, donned fresh clothes, and left as quickly as possible.

She was halfway to the Nathan County Hospital when her phone rang.

"I hope I didn't wake you," Savannah's excited voice said.

"The highway patrol frowns on those who sleep while driving. I'm on the way back to the hospital." Alarm crept up her spine like a spider. "What's up? Is everything all right?"

"They have just taken Cornelia for tests, but I have something to tell you."

"I'm listening."

"No. Face-to-face. How soon can you be here?"

"Without breaking any speed limits, I should be there in about ten minutes. And by the way, *I* have something to tell *you*."

"Oh?"

"Yes, but I'll tell you when I get there."

When Jillian arrived, Savannah was waiting for her just inside the hospital entrance, her face flushed, her eyes dancing.

"What on earth?" Jillian said.

Savannah grabbed her arm and practically hauled her back outside to a bench well away from other activity. Sunshine streamed through the branches of a Bradford pear tree and laid dappled shadows over the two women.

"What is going on?" Jillian asked, her patience straining.

"After Cornelia woke up, she was in a talkative mood."

"That's not hard to believe. She's always—"

"Hush and let me tell you. She talked a little bit about what had happened with Charmaine and all that, but then she wanted to talk about Kandi. How sweet the girl is, and how much fun, and how kind. She went on and on about how they love the same music and books, and how Kandi had read out loud to her yesterday after she shut herself away in her room."

Jillian tamped down that annoying spark of petty jealousy that tried to flare up. If Cornelia wanted someone to read aloud to her, her own great-niece could do that very well.

Savannah leaned closer to Jillian, eyes flashing. "She said how much Kandi loves animals, how Possum was nutty over her, sitting on her lap or nuzzling her. She said, at one point, the girl got down on the floor with the cat and—now here's the good part—Kandi said, 'I bet you're glad no one ever shuts you outside like they did Dipsy Doodle. You'll never have to go running from one door to another trying to get inside with no one there to let you in.'"

Savannah sat back and looked at Jillian expectantly.

"But what's so . . . Wait a minute," Jillian said, frowning. "Repeat that."

Savannah did and watched as Jillian digested the words.

"But Kandi didn't show up until *after* the murder. I never heard anyone tell her about Dipsy Doodle, not even last night at the supper table while we were talking about Charmaine's murder." She thought about it a moment longer. "Unless, of course, Aunt Cornelia filled her in yesterday while they were together."

"That's my thinking exactly. I asked Cornelia if she'd told Kandi about Dipsy Doodle being out all night, and she said, 'No. I'm not much of a dog person, you know.'"

"So then how did Kandi know about the dog? As far as I know, she was with us all the time, cooking and cleaning and serving food."

"Right."

Jillian pondered for a minute. "Now that I think about it, Kandi is a little weird, isn't she? She says she wants to put the story about Charmaine's murder on her blog. That seemed really odd to me. Why would she not write it for her newspaper and get paid for it?"

Savannah got out her phone and started tapping.

"And she seemed far more interested in learning how to tat and make apple pie than getting information like the other reporters had done," Jillian continued. "I mean, they were annoying."

"I thought she was being sweet."

"And if she was such an animal lover, why didn't she and Dipsy Doodle get along?" "Here it is. Her blog. *Kandi Kerber's Eye on the World*."

"For real?"

Savannah showed Jillian the screen.

"And look. She has exactly thirty-four subscribers." She scrolled through the woman's blog. "There are no comments on anything she's written."

"That means either no one is reading them, or no one is interested enough to comment."

"Or maybe no one has taken the time to comment." Savannah frowned as she scrolled and read. "I have to admit, these are badly written."

"Misspelled words?"

"Oh, yes." Savannah sounded pained. She glanced up. "How'd you know that?"

"Because of the note she left behind."

"Huh?"

"Kandi left last night or maybe early this morning. And the note she wrote for us wasn't exactly what a reporter would write."

"And she left, boom? Just like that? No warning, nothing?"

Jillian shook her head.

"It's odd, especially when you consider how she fawned all over Bertie and Cornelia."

"I half-expected her to move in with us. Oh, don't look at me like that. I'm kidding. But she did seem awfully desperate to get close to Bertie and Aunt Cornelia."

"Maybe she was lonely. Maybe she has no family of her own."

"Possibly. But that doesn't explain why she'd suddenly leave. I mean, in the short time she'd been with her, Kandi absolutely doted on Aunt Cornelia. She even referred to Bertie as 'Grandma Bertie.' But she ups and leaves when Aunt Cornelia goes into the hospital."

"Peculiar."

"Very."

For a time, scenes and snippets of conversation rolled through Jillian's mind.

"Hey!" Savannah said suddenly. "At the supper table, Bertie said something about they'll find out she was killed with garden scissors—"

"And Aunt Cornelia dropped her glass, and Kandi choked . . ."

"At first I thought she was startled by the broken dishes. But what if she was the one who killed Charmaine—and she knew she was murdered with scissors." Savannah's voice built with excitement.

"But why would she? As far as we know, the two women had never met."

"Be that as it may, the fact that she knew about Dipsy Doodle being left outside proves she had to have been there and seen it for herself."

"You're right."

"Which means she knows way more than she's telling."

"Or that she killed Charmaine."

"We have no evidence, just our own suspicions," Savannah said.

"That's true. But don't you think we ought to at least talk to Sheriff Henderson? I mean, I'm sure Kandi isn't even on his radar, coming in late like she did and with that slew of reporters. He's not looking at any of them, I'm sure." She blew out a deep breath. "Right now, he's looking at Bryce."

Savannah gasped. "No!"

"Yes."

"But Bryce couldn't . . . wouldn't . . . Well, would he? Do you think he would?"

There was no denying that after the initial shock of Charmaine's death, he changed. Gone was the drawn face, haunted eyes, lifeless expression. He had appeared healthier, almost happy.

"The last time I talked with Bryce, he seemed to be in the process of shedding his grief. Quickly."

Savannah frowned. "I'd hate to think that he killed her. I like him."

"I know you do. But let's not forget that strange man whose very name upset Aunt Cornelia. Something about that man has upset her."

"We should get to the bottom of that, Jillian. In fact, while I have my phone out, I'll do a little checking on him myself." She tapped for a bit, then read what came up on her screen. "Aha."

"Aha? Aha what?"

"Right here. An article in a small newspaper about the celebration of Arthur Fremont's eighty-fifth birthday a year ago. Listed as one of the guests was his niece, Kandi Karen Kerber."

She handed the phone to Jillian, who read the article, her mouth open in amazement.

"Savannah, something definitely stinks. Let's get to the sheriff's office, *now.*"

By the following evening, Cornelia was home, snug in her own bed. She reclined comfortably, her back against a pile of plump, snowy pillows, her tatting basket nearby. Most of the tests revealed she was basically sound and healthy, and the results of a couple of others would take more time. But Dr. Taylor had been upbeat and optimistic, urging rest and a regular diet.

She seemed as relaxed as Jillian had ever known her to be.

As the sun snuggled its way beneath the horizon and daylight gave over to twilight, Bertie stood near the head of the bed and Savannah sat on the edge. She held Cornelia's soft, cool hand while Jillian delivered the news that Charmaine's murderer had been caught.

"What?" Cornelia sat straight up, staring at Jillian, blue eyes wide. "Repeat that, in case my old ears fooled me."

"It's true, Cornelia. The police caught up with Kandi near the Tennessee line this morning. She confessed immediately."

"I can scarcely believe it."

"Coy came by not more than an hour ago and told us everything."

"Oh my." She sagged against her pillow. "Oh dear. I think you better go ahead and tell me all about it."

Bertie ran a concerned gaze across her. "Are you sure, honey? The story isn't going to change, if you'd rather wait a while."

"Wait? Why should I wait?" She lifted her head from the pillow. "I'm only staying in bed because Dr. Taylor told me to, but it's not going to be an extended stay. I'm not a hothouse flower, you know." Cornelia turned to Jillian. "You tell me, and give it to me straight. My sister will only soft-soap it for me."

"Then I'm going to go make you a pot of tea," Bertie said. "And a sandwich. Dr. Taylor said you've not been eating enough lately."

"Bertie's happiest when she's busy." She watched Bertie leave the room, then looked back to Jillian. "Tell me."

"Let me start by telling you that Bryce has been arrested, but not for anything that happened here. He had nothing to do with this situation, other than being Charmaine's grifting partner through it all."

"Grifting partner? What's that?"

"Scam artists. Tricking people out of money or possessions."

Cornelia's mouth flew open. "You mean he wasn't that woman's personal assistant? She lied about that?"

"She lied about everything, even her name, which was Edna Jo Rollings. She wasn't from Virginia; she was from New Jersey. Bryce's real name isn't Bryce Bellingham; it's Randy Phipps. And they were partners in several scams. That's why he's being extradited to Pennsylvania. That time she mistakenly referred to him as Bryce Birmingham should have alerted me to something like this."

"But you know what touched me?" Savannah said. "How he made sure someone from the sheriff's department got in touch with Jack to take Dipsy Doodle. Bryce loves that little dog, and he knew Jack did too. He might be a scam artist, but he's got a good heart."

Jillian smiled at her friend. "Only someone with a good heart could say that, you ol' softie, you."

Cornelia shifted in the bed and made an impatient gesture. "Tell me the rest, for pity's sake."

"It seems more than anything else, Kandi has wanted to make her mark as a journalist. She wanted to be famous for it."

"Oh, did she?"

"According to her, all she needed was a groundbreaking story and her career would be made. And don't look at me like that. This is what she told the sheriff."

"Go on."

"Her uncle knew this about her. So a few nights ago, he told her about some correspondence between Abraham Lincoln and John Wilkes Booth that was hidden somewhere here in Belle Haven."

Cornelia sat straight up. "Arthur Fremont is that girl's uncle? That low-down snake in the grass is her *uncle*?"

"I'm afraid so."

"That was the same story he told Charmaine, isn't it?" Savannah put in.

"Yes, and she believed it. That's why she showed up here. It's why they both showed up here."

Cornelia waved one hand as if brushing away flies.

"Kandi is young and callow, so it's easy to see why she was taken in," Cornelia said. "Charmaine was a ninny, but I would think even a ninny would have more sense than to believe such a wild tale."

Bertie returned with an egg-salad sandwich, but Cornelia wasn't interested in food right then.

"Go on, Jillian," she said.

"Bryce told Coy Henderson that Arthur courted Charmaine for a while. He pursued her quite ardently until he—like Jack Porter—realized she was only after his money and assets."

Cornelia narrowed her eyes. "Unless he's changed, that man has no money. Or assets. He drifts from woman to woman, using up everything she has until there's nothing left." She drew her lips together in a thin line as if she'd never speak again. She gestured for Jillian to continue.

"Coy caught up with Arthur. He was at the Raindrop Motel."

"I didn't know that awful old place was still up and running," Cornelia growled.

"He admitted everything that Bryce and Kandi had said were true. He said he made up the story to pay back Charmaine for taking him for every penny he had—"

"Which was probably about twenty cents. But go on."

"—and he told Kandi the same tale about the letters so she'd come down here and pester Charmaine. It was all a big joke to him."

"But why pick on Belle Haven?" Savannah asked. "There are plenty of other places, much closer to any of them than Moss Hollow."

"Because he wanted to get even with Aunt Cornelia for jilting him. And he came down here to rub it in her face."

Cornelia placed the fingers of both hands against her lips as if she were afraid of what might come out of her mouth. "Oh, that rotten, rotten Arthur," she said at last. "The biggest liar in the world. He caused this, every last bit of it."

"I wouldn't go so far as to say that," Savannah said, her voice quietly comforting. "He might have gotten the ball rolling, but he probably did not intend such a dire result."

"He never thought. Period," Cornelia said. "Even as an old man who ought to know better, Arthur apparently only thinks of Arthur."

"So you knew him quite well?"

"Far too well."

"You've never mentioned him. Not one time." Bertie managed to sound annoyed and hurt at the same time. "I thought you and I always told each other everything."

Cornelia met her eyes. "There are some things best left unsaid. I never told anyone about Arthur." She turned to Jillian. "Go on, please."

"Kandi showed up late that night, during a lull in all that rain. She was snooping around in the back gardens when Charmaine came outside with Dipsy Doodle. Kandi approached her, told her who she was and what she wanted. Apparently, Charmaine had a buyer for the documents, and she wasn't about to let anything mess that up. In fact, she was so furious, it scared Kandi, who remembered seeing the garden scissors on the porch of the shed. She got them and held them as protection when she told Charmaine either to make a deal with her or she'd tell you and Bertie everything."

"Uh-oh."

"When Kandi threatened to reveal all, Charmaine flew into a rage and came at her. Her feet slid in the mud and she fell onto Kandi. And onto the scissors."

Cornelia stared at her a moment, her blue eyes wide. "I knew it. I knew that dear little girl couldn't hurt a fly."

The other three exchanged looks.

"Cornelia," Bertie said, "she was here to get her hands on those letters—"

"*Phony letters!*"

"But she didn't know that," Bertie said. "She was here to get them, not to be our friend or our helper. She was trying to use us, like Charmaine was using us."

"Oh, but—"

"And she left Dipsy Doodle outside instead of finding the poor little thing some shelter."

"And she left Charmaine to die," Jillian added. "If she was such a good person, she would have called for help."

Cornelia shrank back against her pillows as the truth sank in. She turned to stare out at the darkening sky through her window.

"What I'm going to tell you must not leave this room," she said. "If you go sharing this with the Sweetie Pies, I will pack up and move to New South Wales where no one knows me." She passed a look to all three of them.

"You know none of us would ever betray your confidence, Sister."

"Of course not, Aunt Cornelia."

"Never." Savannah's firm voice underscored the promise.

A short silence followed, then she said, "Years ago, before I even met Raymond, I went to a spring dance and met Arthur. He swept me off my feet. Older, handsome, charming, dressed like a million bucks, he had every girl in the place calf-eyed. I was thrilled he wanted me. We had such a good time together. I didn't mind those times when he forgot his wallet. I was happy to pay, especially as it seemed we were heading for matrimony. And then . . ."

She stopped speaking as if her throat had closed. The others looked at her in alarm, but she shook her head and waved away their concern.

"And then I found out he was *already* married. Married! I had been going out with a married man." She covered her face. "The humiliation. The shame. I thought I'd never get over it. I saw him one last time, and that was to tell him if he ever came around me again, I'd go straight to his wife, his parents, and his friends." She dropped her hands. "I found out a few months later that he was a low-down womanizer. A gigolo. A married one, without a penny to call his own, who lived off his wife and her family. I hadn't seen or heard from him again until this past week."

"Oh, honey," Bertie said, sitting on the edge of the bed and gathering Cornelia into her arms. "How in the world did all this happen without me knowing?"

"It happened while you were off on that cooking thing with those people in college. I think it had to do with chef training or something."

"I'm so sorry I wasn't here for you then."

"Don't be. I survived, didn't I?" She wiped away her tears and sat up straight. Possum jumped up on the bed, and Cornelia stroked his soft coat. "Not long after, I met Raymond, and he's never left me. Not really."

"Aunt Cornelia." Jillian crawled across the bed and cuddled the woman. She kissed a damp cheek. "You are the best great-aunt in the world. You know that, don't you?"

Cornelia patted her arm. "I try."

"And if you ever want me to read aloud to you, I'll do it." The two shared a soft laugh.

"I might take you up on that. To be honest, Kandi was a terrible reader. She stumbled over words—a lot." She lowered her voice as if the woman was in the room with them. "I wondered how she could write when she had such trouble reading."

Jillian rested her head against Cornelia's shoulder the way she once had as a child. The comfort she found there was the same.

"She's Arthur's niece, you said."

"Yes, ma'am."

A long sigh traveled from Cornelia's lips. "It runs in the family then, doesn't it? Deceit. Cruelty. Using people."

"So it would seem," Bertie agreed.

"Something else runs in families," Savannah said. "You know what it is?"

They all turned to her. "What?"

"Exactly what I see in this room. Truth. Loyalty. Love."

"Group hug!" Cornelia said from her place on the bed. She held out both arms to include her three companions.

"Now, my dear sister," Bertie said when they came up for air, "eat this sandwich, then it's time for your pills."

"More pills?" Cornelia all but squawked.

"Yes, your vitamins. Your iron supplement and a nice, mild relaxant so you can get a good night's sleep."

Cornelia scowled and clamped her mouth tight.

"If our dear old friend and trusted physician tells us to take them, we take them. Doc Taylor has never steered us wrong."

Cornelia glowered at her.

Bertie glowered back. "If you don't take them, you'll have to stay in bed all weekend and miss the Sweetie Pies meeting. Is that what you want?"

"Why are you always so bossy?"

"Because I'm the oldest and you have to do what I say."

Savannah turned her amused snort into a discreet cough.

Cornelia reached out one hand and accepted the vitamin tablet, the mineral supplement, and the mild relaxant. She swallowed all three at once with a huge gulp of water and gave Bertie back the glass.

She plucked a bit at the coverlet and adjusted it a fraction, then looked up and gave her sister a sheepish smile. "Thank you, dear."

"You're welcome, honey." Bertie leaned over and kissed her cheek.

"I love you," they said to each other in unison.

"See?" Savannah said, smiling at Jillian. "It runs in families."

Honey Dipped Secrets
Book Four Recipe

Bertie's Gone to Heaven Cookies

1 cup shortening
1 cup white sugar
1 cup brown sugar
2 beaten eggs
2 teaspoons vanilla
1½ cups flour
1 teaspoon baking powder

1 teaspoon baking soda
1 teaspoon salt
1½ cups uncooked oatmeal
1½ cups crispy rice cereal
1 cup coconut
1 cup chocolate chips

Instructions

Preheat oven to 350 degrees.

1. Cream together shortening, white sugar, and brown sugar. Add eggs and vanilla to mixture and mix well.

2. In a separate bowl, sift flour, baking powder, baking soda, and salt. Add to creamed mixture, mixing well.

3. Stir in oatmeal, cereal, coconut, and chocolate chips. The mixture will be rather dry.

4. Drop batter by teaspoon 2 inches apart onto ungreased cookie sheet, and bake for 10 to 12 minutes.

5. This is a versatile recipe that can have nuts, peanut butter chips, or other fixings. Reduce or add according to your family's preferred tastes.